# Boris Thinks I'm Funny.

Caution: Foreign relations may cause laughter.

## J.P. Robideaux

Book and cover design by Kevin Breen
Cover image derived from Adobe Stock photos

ISBN: 979-8-218-31458-3
Cataloging-in-Publication Data is available upon request

Manufactured in the United States of America

Published by Deep Breath
The author may be contacted at
johnprobideaux@gmail.com

Other novels by J.P. Robideaux

*Escape Into Rain*
*It's Reigning in London*

"I grew up with six brothers. That's how I learned to dance—waiting for the bathroom."

–Bob Hope

# Chapter 1

LATE MARCH 1993 - RUSSIA - THE KREMLIN

His limo driver rushed through the dusty streets, driving too fast for the conditions, hoping to make the pick up on time. He'd been expecting the call for days, but when it came, he couldn't believe it was actually happening. The driver fought to keep his emotions in check as he wondered where they would end up, North Africa, Italy or Spain? He'd always wanted to see the Rock of Gibraltar, so Spain or Portugal were his hopeful guesses.

The boxy black and silver oversized sedan wasn't meant to be driven faster than passengers could comfortably ride. Denis had to keep a sharp eye out for deepening potholes and fragments of exploded bombs and other debris. He prayed the suspension would hold up as the Russian-made limo sailed over ruts and broken glass, challenging both driver and vehicle beyond their appointed limits.

He'd removed the Presidential flags from the fenders as instructed, and emptied the spacious trunk of all unnecessary items, including several cases of vodka. The call was expected, but expectations can sometimes camouflage reality, Denis thought to himself as he avoided main streets, again as instructed. This style of driving ran counter to his normal requests from President Yeltsin - *to drive slowly so his people could see the man who led them into prosperity.*

One more corner and across a six laned, uneven, main street intersection and the fast-moving target finally would be able to slow down. The last maneuver nearly sent the former world-class weightlifter into the windshield. The professional bodyguard and driver made it into a narrow and secluded back alleyway. When he was finally able to slow down, Denis took a breath, smiled to himself, and sat back as he began to relax a little. He wiped his sweaty palms on his pants as he avoided the occasional pothole. Denis looked into the rearview mirror. A feeling of satisfaction came over him. Once in a while, Denis enjoyed the rush of driving fast past crowds on thoroughfares that had been blocked off for the President's convoy. But not today. His smile began to fade as he remembered those times, but his confidence remained strong, that part of him would always remain. He knew he was in a race for his life and that of the man he hurried to pick up. The two were inseparable. Denis had pledged an oath that equaled his loyalty to his own family — those that he would also take a bullet for.

Driving the alleyways required a different set of skills. Missed-placed cobblestones became projectiles that plunked up against the undercarriage of the car as if being tossed from underground. Potholes turned into craters camouflaged by puddles inflicting harsh punishment on poorly manufactured struts and shocks. He slowed the long, low riding black Zil 117, his pride and joy, trying to avoid debris that fell from the sides of buildings damaged by bullets and explosives. Denis disliked driving this rarely used route, but quickly changed his attitude as he parked as directed, adjacent to a service door beneath the shadowed safety of an overhanging balcony.

He radioed his arrival to the Colonel of the Guard and waited, motor running - his chambered service revolver in his lap, eyes taking turns monitoring the rearview mirrors and looking straight ahead, waiting for the service door to open. The pulsating rhythm of his heart became more prominent the longer he sat, but he knew how to deal with moments such as this. Denis learned to conquer his fears years ago in the military as a Spetsnaz Commando. Looking back in the mirror reminded him of those times and how far he had come with the man he would guard with his life and his trusted Makarov semi-automatic. He heard something and shifted his gaze forward toward movement and footsteps as he brought his pistol up to his chest.

Two men appeared at the service door, flung it open, and ran for the limo. Denis waited impatiently as they threw luggage in the open trunk and slammed the lid. The slam caused Denis to cringe as he shifted forward in his seat.

He received instructions on his radiophone to drive the men to the more familiar underground garage as they settled in the back. Denis didn't question the order for the short drive or look at the men at first, choosing to drive to the garage, twenty meters ahead. He could tell by the sound that the men in the back were checking their loaded handguns. The mood in the limo grew tense as Denis made a turn.

The limo hit bottom with a loud scraping noise, sending the passengers up off their seats. "Sorry, tight corner, big car."

The sound made Denis flinch as he checked the rearview mirror once again. His passengers stared straight ahead, choosing not to respond, with stoic looks that could kill. They reminded him of grim people on a bus waiting for the next stop while hanging onto the side straps overhead. The limo's headlights automatically illuminated as the drive became narrow and darker.

The stream of light from the headlights appeared to pull them forward into a dark cave, like a dusty rope being yanked by a mysterious stranger. The chatter from the concrete against the tires nearly drowned out one of the men as he shouted out an order: "Second level stairway, keep the motor running!"

§

President Yeltsin's drunken sleep came to an abrupt halt. Loud snoring gave way to shouts and yelling when he hit his head on the bedpost in an attempt to sit up. Luka, his personal aide, rushed to dress the half-naked leader. "Where are you taking me, what's happening, Luka?"

"We haven't much time, sir, we must hurry."

Men, loyal to the President, waited in the half-lit hallway outside the leader's bedroom suite. Colonel Sergey Baskin looked at his watch through beads of sweat that ran down his face and into a full salt and pepper beard. The Colonel had been notified, just minutes before, at 2am, that a coup had been announced over government radio. Tanks close to the Presidential Headquarters, known, ironically, as the White House, would be rolling soon creating a barrier, making an escape almost impossible. Those opposed to Boris Yeltsin would be coming for the man who they believed was mostly responsible for the dismantling of the USSR and moving Russia into a devastating financial crisis. A judicial warrant for his arrest had been declared in the announcement, and those close to the President, who resisted, had been shot or arrested.

Because of Yeltsin's lingering drunken state, he was placed heavily into a wheelchair as eight armed men went into action. They swept him down the hall and into an elevator. Four ran ahead clearing the way armed with AK-47s as two officers guided the wheelchair with two other men running behind, making sure no one followed. Once they reached the main floor his wheelchair turned into a gurney as they tilted the man back and half carried the nearly three-hundred-pound load down to the second level of the parking garage.

The two men awaiting the Russian President could hear the soldiers struggling before they appeared at the bottom. Denis heard them, too, as he stood by the open trunk. He recognized one of the men waiting, Dimitri Anotonov, a former KGB Bureau Chief, who introduced Denis to the second man, an American, Bernard Jackson with the CIA. Both men would be responsible for President Yeltsin from this moment until his hopeful return.

"Arrangements have been made for you, Denis," Anotonov calmly said as they loaded two medium sized suitcases and a backpack into the trunk.

"You will be accompanying the President. Call your wife and let her know you are on a mission. No details beyond that, you understand? Let her know she will be notified, later today, regarding relocation plans for her and your family until your return." Denis nodded his head. He knew only to obey and not to ask any questions in that hurried moment.

He closed the lid of the trunk carefully, re-entered the limo, and made the call on his radiophone.

For the past several months, Yeltsin had been directing his associates to initiate directives that would ultimately change the course of the countries affected by the breakup of the USSR into "smaller pieces." His vision for Russia appeared to be shared by men like Vladimir Putin, one of his most trusted and loyal associates. "We will one day become a more open society, enabling each citizen to take part in making decisions for themselves as they prosper," Yeltsin had been recently quoted in the media.

That statement, along with other selected visions of how life could be, did not sit well with the established communist government in Moscow. The United States of America's government took notice and a piece of history that had been kept secret until that moment, was put into action.

The plan that President Boris Yeltsin would disappear for a short period of time, saving his life and aiding him in his quest to redirect former USSR policies, had been given the greenlight. Yeltsin was heralded as a courageous leader to many in the country, outside of Russia, and around the world. His plans for inclusion into Western society would change Russian life for the better. And although the previous years of his life had been beyond stressful for him and his family, he never lost his sense of humor.

"Where are we going, Denis? I don't feel like working out this morning. In fact, I could use some aspirin. Who are you, sir?" Yeltsin looked around the limo as they headed back out into the streets of Moscow. He sat back, staring at the black man sitting across from him dressed in dark, casual clothing. The man had a military look about him as they traded glances. No one said a word as the limo came to an intersection where two more vehicles joined in the escape. Yeltsin noticed as his head slowly began to clear. He suddenly felt the need to say something. Looking at Dimitri and then back to the man across from him, Yeltsin offered; "I couldn't help but notice your watch, sir." Jackson smiled, introduced himself, and removed the black-faced Breitling Professional Endurance watch with the salmon-colored band. Yeltsin nodded to the man in appreciation after taking the watch and giving it the once over. Yeltsin handed the oversized watch back to the man as the caravan made several turns at various speeds, causing the three men to move side-to-side.

"I can tell from your watch it is time to leave."

# Chapter 2

1993 - SPOKANE, WASHINGTON - CITY HALL

His desk faced an exterior window, the only confirmation of weather conditions that seemingly changed more often than his daily routine. Jack Templeman sat, working diligently, as he always did, on another set of land development plans according to the city's master plan. After a decade in this department, Jack had worked his way up to Chief Planner, the top spot in his department. His goal had been to achieve the coveted job position before his fortieth birthday. He still had another year to go, which made him feel he'd reached the top of the mountain sooner than expected. Jack wanted to do more climbing and possibly find new vistas. A far-off thought became prominent as he sat at his drafting table. working through the developer's proposed site lines. *I have to take time to set new goals for myself.*

When he first entered the job, twelve years ago, he was filled with optimism, ideas and energy. Jack grew up in Spokane and was ready to be part of making the Lilac City, aptly named because of the hoard of lilac varietals that dotted the community, even more beautiful. After all, he and his, then, new bride, Ellen, lived in God's country, the Pacific Northwest. The land of outdoor recreation, Nordstrom, Starbucks, Boeing, Mariners, Seahawks, and so many start-up companies. More specifically, Spokane was located in the furthest eastern part of the State of Washington known as the Inland Empire. Less than a two-hour drive from the Canadian border to the north, and a half hour from Idaho to the east, Spokane offered four seasons of enjoyment for people of all ages. Jack would often use reminiscing thoughts of his hometown in creating development plans for the future. He looked at the new set of plans before him and promised himself to make this new housing development even more attractive, as he cracked his knuckles and started his day.

"Morning, Jack." The greeting shook Jack out of the stare down he'd been having with the plat map of a fourth addition of the West Plains subdivision known as: Sunset West. Without looking up he returned the greeting and focused at the sheets on his drafting table. His goal on the first three additions had been to work more with the land by saving forested areas and large basalt outcroppings. The developer was reluctant, at first, to work with Jack's ideas because of the added expense. But eventually gave in because of Jack's urging and agreed to work with the city. The development sold out in record time. Since then, the developer, among several others who had a similar experience, has appreciated working with Jack's department.

Jack's challenges used to be something to look forward

to, especially in the winter prior to spring construction. But recently Jack was finding it harder and harder to get excited about right of ways, street lighting, and greenbelts. He wondered if it was just a phase or if he made the wrong decision in choosing his current occupation? The more he thought about it the more his back ached. He'd come into the office early and had been sitting too long. Jack had to move and stretch, refill his coffee, and see who else had arrived.

"Morning, Ed."

"Jack, you're here early. Hey, coach, how'd your youth soccer games go this weekend?"

"Unbelievable, Ed. The Green Machine hasn't lost yet. Our, ten and eleven year – old, kids are really playing well together. I feel like we have a target on our backs though. The games have been close, with even better teams on the schedule for next week. Practices this week are going to be longer." Ed could tell that Jack enjoyed working with *his kids*.

Jack and Ellen decided to wait on having children, but the clock was ticking on that decision. Instead, they decided to donate time to mentor children, coaching soccer happened to be a passion they both shared. Ellen assists by organizing snacks with the moms and acting as team medical advisor. Most of the people in Jack's office enjoy hearing about his coaching challenges, especially Ed.

The two men reviewed their weekend exploits over coffee. Jack and Ed are neighbors and carpool three days a week to their downtown office at City Hall. They are the best of friends and watch each other's backs, especially when the Mayor, Ira Walters, or one of his subordinates, comes sniffing around.

The mayor has a mix of particular, or rather peculiar, idiosyncrasies, which cause him, in Jack's and Ed's opinion, to be one of the most annoying people on the face of the earth. Topping the list would be his need to appear to be everybody's friend. Each workday, both Jack and Ed did their best to be unavailable when the mayor called from the seventh floor, five floors above the Planning Department's skywalk level. Monday, however, was the one day there is no escaping the mayor's 9 a.m. "Gathering of the Minds," meeting. The purpose of the gathering was to prepare the Mayor for the City Council meeting held every Monday evening at 6 p.m. sharp, except for holidays and the months of July and August, during vacation time. It always bothered Jack that the Mayor and City Council got some relief from their jobs during the summer, but not any other departments in City Hall. Add inconsistent management to the mayor's list of idiosyncracies, which also included; bad cigar breath and the occasional failure to stay awake during the city's cable television coverage of council meetings. The last idiosyncrasy led Jack to nickname various administration officials after Disney's Seven Dwarfs. Mayor Walters became: Sleepy.

Jack and Ed headed to the elevator with the new subdivision plans carefully rolled up under Ed's arm and the scale model, on a three by two-foot-wide board, carried by Jimmy, a journeyman planner. They had three minutes to make the Monday meeting on time, but neither Jack or Ed seemed to be in any hurry. Ed held the elevator door for Jimmy and a few stragglers rushing to join them. Jack had his notes that he reviewed as he waited for the doors to close. He would be making a presentation to the group concerning the new subdivision and an update on a new computer graphics system Ed had been researching. That new system would cut their work time in half, but the cost required an increase in their capital budget. Jack was confident he could *wow the crowd*, at least, that's how he viewed his time in the spotlight. He wouldn't need more than fifteen minutes for both subjects, unless his audience needed some warm-up jokes. He'd brought some just in case. He would study the room first, before utilizing a joke or two.

"Let's see, model board, plans and jokes, right, Jack"? Ed knew Jack better than he knew himself, which meant Jack would make yet another attempt to break up the meeting with some unexpected comments that invariably would lead to laughter. "Jokes?" Jimmy said as he shifted his weight trying to keep the scale model level. "Yes, Jimmy. Jokes. Some people love them and others really need them. This is a time of need, trust me," Jack stated as he raised a finger to the sky in false drama as a big smile appeared. Some laughter could be heard from others as they exited on the fifth floor.

The hallway leading to the mayor's meeting room was long and dark. It reminded Jack of corridors seen in horror movies. The door to the conference room was open, glasses were being filled with water as the men entered. They were among the last to join the gathering, which on that day included twenty-five department heads and a few invited guests. Jack felt a sense of pride when he saw Mayor Walters checking his watch and looking up at Jack with a face full of disdain for his unruly department head.

"Well, it's good to see that the Planning Department is right on time. Jack, Ed, and who?" The mayor's assistant leaned over and whispered a name. "Ah, yes, James." Sit gentlemen, let's get started. Rebecca, my assistant will now read the minutes from the last meeting." Jack made a few, last minute, changes to his notes as Rebecca, nickname: Bashful, wound through the high points of the last meeting. One of the highlights was the "Bring a child to work day."

Rebecca smiled as she shared how her son enjoyed his time at City Hall, and complimented the mayor even though the special day had been in force long before Mayor Walter's term. Jack had to laugh remembering how Dash, his white Westie, enjoyed *his* time at City Hall, chasing the janitor and pooping in the elevator - twice. To his amazement, there was no mention of the cute little Westie who managed to take over the Planning Department that day. When she completed her task, Rebecca returned to her seat, turning the meeting back over to the mayor.

"Good morning, everyone. You all look so bright and ready to greet the day. We have a full agenda and a request from our ever-efficient Planning Department. Jack Templeman and his associates would like to make their presentation at the beginning of the meeting, which, seeing no objections, will happen. But first, I want to make an announcement. My wife, Estelle, will be co-chairing a very important event with me this year." Some rumbling and a few coughs could be heard as the mayor turned over his note card, looked over his reading glasses and continued. "Good. Ah, let's see. I know you're all excited."

Jack rolled his eyes as Ed looked at his feet trying not to laugh as Jack wrote Estelle's nickname, Grumpy, on a napkin. Jimmy just looked at the mayor wide-eyed. "Yes, well, together, Estelle and I will head up Riverfront Park's Spring Fling in May." Rebecca encouraged some polite applause and a few oohhs and aahhs came from the people gathered around the large table. "Thank you, thank you. It promises to be a fun time with more information to come in a few weeks."

Once the Mayor finished, Jack walked over to a podium at the front of the room while Jimmy and Ed set the scale model of the new housing development on the desk next to the mayor and his assistant.

The two returned to their seats at the opposite end of the room. Jack waited patiently for Ed and Jimmy to sit before beginning. He watched the mayor shift in his seat. Jack knew the man liked to keep things going and hated to wait for anyone for any reason.

"Thank you, Mr. Mayor. I believe I speak for all of us when I say that we look forward to whatever you and your lovely wife decide to "fling" at us this Spring. One person spit coffee back into their mug as others covered their mouths trying not to laugh. Jack, being Jack, could not help but interject a joke. The moment was perfect. "Oh, and by the way, sir. I understand maintenance has completed the removal of your home phone number from the third and fourth floor restroom walls. Along with the disgusting graffiti suggesting a "Good Time." A stunned silence dropped from above as the mayor's face changed color to a deep red. The only sound that could be heard was from Rebecca's pen scribbling a notation frantically. Jack adjusted his notes and began the presentation by introducing his cohorts.

"Joining me this morning are two of my associates, Jimmy, a junior at Eastern Washington University. Jimmy is a journeyman planner, attending his first Monday meeting with the mayor, and is one of our newer members, poor fella." More laughs, and a few lingering looks from young ladies sitting close by, for the tall handsome young man with dark curly hair and a perfect smile. "And most of you know Ed La Drew, Assistant Chief in the Department." Both raised their hands as they were introduced.

The presentation went well and the three planners were on their way before the hour was out. Jack hardly ever stayed for the entire meeting anymore. The mayor wasn't happy about Jack's request to go first, but acknowledged that there was less tension in the room after Jack and his people left. One year Jack left a whoopie cushion on the mayor's chair after the highest-ranking official at City Hall left the meeting for a moment. Employees who witnessed the mayor's embarrassing bout with the cushion upon his return to the meeting still talk about the incident, which made Jack even more popular.

As a form of celebration, Jimmy left for Starbucks after dropping the model off with the design team on the second floor. He was on his normal mission: Monday morning - *glad we didn't have to stay in the mayor's meeting lattes*, which included one for Jimmy. The journeyman planner wannabe enjoyed deviating from his regular job to go to Starbucks, besides, it gave him a chance to flirt with the female baristas. He used his curly dark afro to great advantage as he ordered two Americanos with room for cream and a Frappuccino for himself.

Jack's Monday's included time preparing for and attending the evening City Council meeting, but not tonight. He gave the honor to Ed, who reluctantly agreed to fill-in for Jack. After all, it was Jack's anniversary, lucky number thirteen. Jack considered himself to be one of the lucky ones, so this anniversary was even more special, attempting to top last year. That thought of going above and beyond had been lingering for weeks, but he'd put it off, until now. Anniversary card from a cute floral shop, along with orange roses, perfume from Nordstrom, dinner reservations, check, check, and check. Jack wasn't satisfied, he needed one more thing, and that thought was top of mind as he drove out of the parking garage to do some grocery shopping.

Ellen Templeman entered the nurses' locker room at the medical center humming to Abba's "Dancing Queen" Ellen had just completed her shift in the hospital's Neonatal Intensive Care Unit or NICU. Her Critical Care Registered Nurse status allowed Ellen to work with some of the most vulnerable patients, babies born fighting for their lives or needing more time to develop before being discharged. Ellen felt her work in the NICU gave her so much more than she could ever provide in return. The low-lit atmosphere with soft conversation surrounded the staff of dedicated individuals who worked around the clock to provide the latest treatments available.

One of her associates interrupted as Ellen's humming continued. "Hey, Dancing Queen. Are you off duty?" Ellen, surprised by her colleague's greeting, returned to humming, then turned and smiled as she happily announced; "Yes, and it's our thirteenth anniversary, Shelly." Congratulations and goodbyes were exchanged by Shelly and a few others that overheard their conversation.

Ellen exited the room heading home to meet Jack before going out to dinner at a new restaurant that Ellen hoped he had remembered to make reservations to, as she'd requested. Ellen had a smile on her face and a skip in her step as she walked to her car. Her attitude was also heightened by the fact that she also had the next three days off. "Hello, car."

Jack stood in the kitchen, by the center island, reading the mail when Ellen entered through the laundry room. The television news provided background noise with the latest "breaking report" flashing on the screen. Dash, their pure-bred white Highland Westie, crunched away at his dog dish near the slider leading to the backyard. This was their routine. Jack normally arrived home first, fed the dog, checked the mail right around news time. But today promised to be different. Anniversaries take precedence over routines.

"Hey, mister." Jack looked up and smiled at her. "Hi, Sweetheart." They embraced, kissed, as Jack kissed Ellen one more time on the forehead, held her by the shoulders and, looking her straight in the eyes, said, "I have some great news." Ellen was ready for what she thought could be information related to their anniversary celebration. It was up to Jack to make reservations at the restaurant, It's Thyme, and she really hoped he remembered. "Lay it on me, Jack." He carefully moved Ellen down onto a bar stool. He then proceeded to pull a cream-colored card out of his back pocket, like a magician about to perform an amazing trick. The card had the City's logo on it, but Ellen couldn't tell what it said because Jack kept waving it. He suddenly stopped and announced "Our home value is higher than we expected."

It took a few beats as Jack kept his straight-faced stare, slight smile including a minor head shake. Finally, he couldn't hold it any longer and began laughing, which caused Ellen to do the same as she pushed him off the bar stool onto the floor where they proceeded to wrestle with Dash pouncing around acting as referee. "You bastard!"

The card and accompanying dozen roses, orange of course, her favorite, were neatly hidden in the next room. Jack had done it. He'd been working on his timing all day. He couldn't stop thinking about how he would surprise her when she came home. Would she be in a good mood? Did she have a good day? He'd decided that playing it low key and throwing her off a little was the best approach. After dinner at their favorite restaurant along the river, they strolled along the waterfront in Riverfront Park, a community favorite place to go and relax. The sun had set, but the light lingered long enough to complete a perfect day. The two love birds walked for another few minutes before heading home. Spring had finally arrived, but the most important thing at the moment superseded the season. Jack and Ellen were entering their 14th year together. Jack promised Ellen that the year would continue to be full of surprises. Good ones.

§

## THULE AIR BASE - GREENLAND

The Russian military aircraft received clearance to land at Thule Air Base in Greenland. The irony of the event was not lost on the U.S. service personnel who were on duty at the time. Thule, for some time, had been a launching point for allied forces working spy missions over various foreign territories, especially Russia.

The plane had been airborne for five hours and planned to refuel before returning to an air base somewhere in Russia – yet to be determined. The CIA arranged for a smaller Gulfstream government plane to meet the Russian President's entourage. The U.S. contingent arrived an hour earlier and were prepared to fly President Boris Yeltsin to an undisclosed destination in the United States the minute he arrived. The special force assigned to this mission wanted to keep on the move, knowing they were part of an historic event.

A special meeting between the CIA and Joint Chiefs of Staff reviewed a number of locations that would be considered far off the international radar, but close enough to monitor on a daily basis. The deep south and southwestern desert country were top considerations until a general, who had spent time in the Pacific Northwest, made a case for the eastern region of Washington State where a large military air force base was located. Knowing that Yeltsin had to be safely protected for possibly a month caused the Pentagon to put their best officers in charge of the mission. Their hope was that the time period the government projected would be limited to just a few weeks. The longer the unrest against Yeltsin, the harder it would be to keep his location a secret. The location that ultimately received a unanimous vote was the Pacific Northwest more specifically, Spokane, Washington.

Although the handoff of a foreign President, seeking asylum, albeit temporary, may have been new to most of the participants involved in the exercise, Jackson and Anotonov had worked on similar clandestine missions. The CIA and KGB had a history of working together for the advancement of each participant's agenda in Africa and South America and behind the scenes with their respective space programs. However, temporarily removing an existing President added a new twist to each man's resume.

Dimitri Antonov wondered to himself how he would be treated if this relocation of Boris Yeltsin somehow became an international incident. The well-trained former KGB Chief had never been to the United States, and was somewhat apprehensive about monitoring the man sitting adjacent to him. He admired Boris Yeltsin and would, if necessary, take a bullet for him. Still, he couldn't let go of the personal concern he had for making this operation work. It all came down to him, as his superior officer explained. If it were known that the United States was involved in protecting Boris Yeltsin, the ramifications could be the cause of an international incident that could lead to World War III.

As they excited the Russian aircraft, Bernard Jackson pulled Dimitri to one side.

"Since this will be your first time in America, let me give you one more piece of advice."

"Don't tell me, become a New York Yankee fan?" "No, that's not where I was going, Dimitri, but now that you mention it, you may want to become a Seattle Mariners fan. "Mariners?" "Yes, Dimitri." You'll be in the Northwest, about as far away as you can get from New York City, my friend."

"Ah, yes, of course. Thank you, Mister Jackson. Do you have any more advice to keep me from making a fool of myself?" Dimitri continued.

"You don't smile much, consequently, you look like a bodyguard. Dead giveaway. Smile more. Force yourself if you have to, does that make sense?" "It's not easy to smile under the circumstances facing us, Mr. Jackson, but I will do my best. Besides, Denis will be, how do you say it? The President's sidekick? I will remain with you monitoring from the shadows. But I will share your sentiment about smiling more with Denis. He and I, along with so many others, suffer from the same condition, Mr. Jackson, fear of repression." Jackson understood and nodded his head as he patted Dimitri on the shoulder.

The men boarded the U.S. government plane and left Greenland before the Russian contingent had finished refueling for their return trip. After the Gulfstream took off, the Russian plane received clearance to be flown to a safe location in Tbilisi, Georgia on the Black Sea. The plan would be to rendezvous at a later date, yet to be determined, back at Thule Air Base.

As the large Russian cargo plane took off, the air traffic control team breathed a sigh of relief as they watched the white dot on the radar move – heading 090.

§

"Jack, you are a nut, you know that, right?" "Of course. Where are you going with this, El?"

"Game night."

"Game night?"

"Yes, listen and retain, Jack. This Saturday, Ed and his wife, and one other couple from the neighborhood, I can't remember their names at the moment, are coming over."

"Got it."

"I'm just warning you, new people, who do not know you and your funny little quirks, will be in attendance. I'll get their names from Janice, but be on your best behavior, please, Jack."

Ellen felt obligated to warn Jack about the newcomers. Whenever they gathered with friends, Jack often, when the mood struck him, turned a friendly gathering into a comedy club. Friends around the table would become his audience, and the show would begin. If the room vibe was a little low, Jack would automatically turn it up. Not that that was a bad thing, most of the time people responded favorably. Ellen just wanted to make sure the newcomers wouldn't suddenly turn and run out the front door.

The week of the get together passed quickly, Ellen had Saturday off, giving her plenty of time to prepare hors d'oeuvres for their game night. She chopped and sliced; carrots, peppers and three kinds of cheeses as she watched the evening news. Jack was working out at the gym and would be home soon. She couldn't help but notice Dash watching the news, intently, as if he hung on every word. *Funny*, she thought and passed it off as nothing more than a rare moment. Ellen made a mental note to tell Jack.

She smiled as she chopped, thinking of Dash while watching the news herself, which happened to be announcing the disappearance of Boris Yeltsin. She reached for the remote and turned the volume up. Dash turned and looked back at her, tailing wagging, as if to say, thanks, then returned to watching. A laugh escaped her as she whispered, "You're welcome, Dash old boy."

*"Boris Yeltsin is believed to be hiding out somewhere in Ukraine, near Kiev. People close to the President were quoted as saying that: "The President fled the region in the last twenty-four hours for his own safety. They would not confirm the exact location, but Yeltsin has been known to visit the region where he grew up. Sources tell us that Yeltsin visited Ukraine several times in the last six months."*

The report showed footage of Yeltsin as he walked near the Kremlin a few days before his disappearance. The reporter went on to say: *"Sources close to the President did say that they did not fear for his life at this time and would release more information at a later date. Meanwhile, the Russian foreign minister met with Communist officials for undisclosed reasons, as tanks moved to block passage in various locations in Moscow."*

Ellen stood amazed as Dash held his gaze on the television longer than she'd thought any dog could. Of course, the Westie breed was known to have something of a sixth sense about life that she and Jack witnessed on occasion. Television watching, singing along with certain music, barking as if talking, and selective food desires like pasta, topped the list of Dash oddities. Dash was very picky about what he ate. Jack enjoyed sharing a funny story about the first time he attempted to introduce regular canned dog food to Dash. "He smelled, backed off, shook his head, looked at me, then walked off. I felt ashamed." Dash also had an uncanny ability to sit and stare until you figured out, either the house was on fire or he had to go out. "If we decide to have children of our own, I hope they grow up to be just like our, independent thinking, Dash," Jack shared with Ellen recently. Their amazing pet eventually lost interest in the news, but not before they ran an old story showing Yeltsin saying a few words in response to what was happening in his nation's capital.

§

## SOMEWHERE OVER MONTANA AIRSPACE

The smaller jet that contained the President of Russia and his entourage cruised at 40,000 feet, heading further west, in more luxury than the previous flight. The smooth ride felt good and allowed everyone to relax as they chased the sun toward the Pacific. Boris asked if the plane had a bar on board. The U.S. government believed good foreign relations were dependent on attention given to every detail, including hospitality. After a brief discussion, vodka martinis were served. Yeltsin, after his first sip, saluted everyone aboard and began to drink to everyone's health. He asked Denis to mix drinks for his fellow passengers and led them in singing, "Patrioticheskaya Pesnya" the national anthem every loyal Russian knew by heart. He and Denis sang while the rest watched, sipped and toasted.

Between the free-flowing vodka and the altitude, the singing became more and more impassioned. By the time the captain began his descent, the singers and the vodka were hoarse and depleted in that order. Quiet came over the plane as a sense of urgency returned.

The American designed Gulfstream not only turned out to be more comfortable than the old Russian military plane, but it had great acoustics. In the silence that followed the singing, the jet descended out of a clear forever sky and into the unwelcome grasp of clouds. Boris watched out his window as the darkening landscape began to reveal itself. Lights were beginning to show as he blinked several times in order to focus. Farmland appeared first, lakes, roads, a huge ribbon of interstate freeway, a city with a river running through it, and buildings. Upon closer review, evergreen trees, specifically, pine, similar to the ones in the northern parts of his homeland were everywhere. *Nice,* he thought to himself as the captain flashed the seatbelt sign and passengers began to stir in their seats.

The plane landed on time at Fairchild Air Force Base and immediately taxied to the far western end of the runway. A three-person contingent stood waiting in an empty, rarely used, hangar. Their sole purpose that evening was to receive the top-secret flight. The hangar doors had been opened wide, making the enormous gray windowless structure resemble a monster ready to devour whatever came near it. The three officials, two State Department and one military, had flown in from Washington D.C., the other Washington involved in this escapade. No one, not even top military officers stationed at the base, knew that the President of Russia would be walking off the clandestine flight.

Bernard Jackson, a good singer in his own right, enjoyed the sing-along, which helped to pass the time. He managed to remain sober enough, as did Denis. Together they deplaned ahead of the other four. Yeltsin, Anotonov, who were feeling no pain as they exited the aircraft, managed to remain upright. They weren't falling down drunk, but they, momentarily, delayed feeling any of the anxiety that surrounded them like a suffocating cloud. Two military guards, who must have considered themselves, unfortunately, on duty during the vodka free-for-all, brought up the rear carrying a small amount of luggage. They will certainly have a story to tell, Jackson thought to himself as the four piled into a large black SUV.

The sun had set on a perfect March evening. Operation Exit, as the U. S. State Department referred to the plan, was now in the Pacific Northwest, in the city of Spokane, Washington, a place that no one onboard had ever considered visiting.

As he peered out the window of the SUV, this location reminded Boris of another land. The President stopped talking in order to hear the driver explain where they were, which, in his current altered state of mind, sounded and looked a lot like his childhood homeland in the Russian countryside. Even as the light continued to fade, he could clearly see pine trees and rock formations. The driver had to momentarily stop talking while he entered into traffic. The sudden silence gave Yeltsin a chance to speak. "This area reminds me of my homeland. We would go on marches, for days, into the wilds that my father, Nikolai, engineered. My siblings and I had so much fun together. Mikhail and Valya would hide among the tallest of trees and I would have to find them."

The driver and the two guards sitting in back listened intently as they headed east on Highway 2 towards the Sunset Hill. The large black SUV merged onto I-90 and the city of Spokane came into full view. Boris suddenly stopped talking as he looked out over the impressive expanse of lights and remarked at how much it reminded him of a small city near Kiev. Within a few minutes they turned at the bottom of the hill and headed onto a smaller highway going south to a place the driver called: Eagle Ridge.

§

Jack and Ellen welcomed their guests as they arrived for game night in their home that evening. It had been Ellen's idea, a couple of years ago, to have people in the neighborhood over to play various games and get to know them better. Jack, with his entertaining spirit, was onboard right away. That's how they became friends with Ed and Janice. Besides, he enjoyed playing games, not necessarily from a competitive perspective, but more about watching people enjoy themselves. From cards to dominoes, board games to Pictionary, the choices were made once the visitors had a drink and something to eat. If anyone hesitated, Ellen would make a suggestion and the games began. That night the evening entertainment began with Pictionary.

Jack brought home his easel board with large sheets of white paper, hoping the group would all agree to play the stand-up team game. Pictionary happened to be his personal favorite. It gave everyone involved an opportunity, especially Jack, to be in the spotlight for three minutes at a time. Once the guests agreed, it was game on. The teams were split evenly, the ladies versus the men, three on each side. Ladies first. Topic cards with names of figures to be drawn were lying face down on the coffee table adjacent to the board. Ed's wife, Janice, went first. Her card read: Bowl of Spaghetti.

Janice knew she had to be careful with Jack and Ed, closely watching every move of the pen. The last time they played, the ladies beat the men three out of four games. She enjoyed playing Pictionary because it gave her a chance to be creative. Janice had been taking art classes at the local community college and couldn't wait to demonstrate some of her newfound skills. *Bowl of Spaghetti, here we go*, she thought to herself and nodded to Jack. Jack turned the three-minute hourglass timer over. "Begin."

Shaking both arms to relax her before beginning, she took a deep breath and went for the easel. The whole pre-draw ceremony didn't go unnoticed by Don and Kate Pierson, the newlywed guests. Jack noticed their moving van last week and boldly invited the young couple before they had completely unpacked. "You bought the Johnson place, good for you. You should join us for game night." Jack was not only funny - he had a bold side. Both newlyweds looked at one another as if they were about to play in the Superbowl of Pictionary, a contest they hadn't expected. They knew the game, but neither had ever felt the tension that now existed in the Templeman's living room.

As Janice moved her marker in flowing lines, her teammates began to yell responses. Jack, Ed and Don sat back, Ed glanced at the hour glass as Janice's strokes became more prominent on the page and shouts of guesses filled the air.

"Snakes. Worms coming out of the ground, Medusa." Janice looked at her teammates and shook her head, and quickly changing strategies, put a big equal sign on the page as Jack shouted: "Two minutes." A heel, then a toe appeared. "Shoe, boot." Janice turned, smiled and urged more from her teammates as she pointed to the equal sign. "Spaghetti in a bowl." "Yes!" Janice shouted. The guys looked at one another with surprised expressions. Ellen had come up with the answer and they couldn't figure out what the equal sign had to do with anything. Jack smiled and whispered to his teammates, "Don't ask guys, just let it go, trust me."

And, so it went. The ladies appearing to play the game as if they had invented it. At one point, Jack stopped the game to ask his teammates if they understood the concept of the game as he was willing to go over the rules one more time with them. All in jest of course. The men went down in flames - laughing and having a good time.

After two hours of Pictionary, the men threw in the towel and declared game over as drinks were refilled before starting Mexican dominoes. As the dominoes were being laid out, Ed asked Jack if he'd seen the new arrival down the street.

"You mean the Miller's house finally sold?" "Must have. How long has it been? Nine months?" "At least," Jack commented as he and Don spread the dominoes out, face down, on the table. Kate spoke up and said that she and Don saw people mowing the backyard of the house on Pinehurst, if that's the one you're talking about. "We went on a walk and saw a small moving van with men placing furniture in the garage later in the evening."

Game night continued until nearly midnight, full of laughter with a competitive spirit that everyone, including the newcomers, enjoyed. Don and Kate walked home satisfied that they had made the right decision by moving to Eagle Ridge. They'd been told that their neighborhood had a reputation of creating close relationships, which they had witnessed firsthand that evening.

§

Boris and Denis sat in the living room of their temporary American home listening to the new protocol provided by the U.S. government. The Russian leader and his driver/ bodyguard would be expected to follow certain procedures once their protectors left and moved into the shadows. For all intents and purposes, they were to appear as new residents of the eastern Washington community of Eagle Ridge located in the city of Spokane. No one involved knew the exact timeframe for the relocation, but a new updated estimate of possibly two months had been projected by both governments involved. Turmoil and chaos reigned down in Moscow and negotiations were at a standstill.

Back in Spokane, every detail had to be handled properly, from the cutting of the grass, garbage collection, to lights on in the house, anything that gave the appearance of a normal residence. The yard would be taken care of by a professional landscaping service, but the rest will be up to Boris and Denis.

March in Spokane doesn't usually require much landscaping, and Denis offered to do any maintenance if necessary. "I am considered to be very helpful at home when lights go out or plumbing backs up." Anotonov smiled at the man's serious expression. Dimitri knew that Denis was more famous for his ability to crush a man's skull or slit a throat as well. At five feet ten inches and weighing just over 200 pounds, the stocky former weightlifter could handle more than changing a light bulb. The blonde forty-year-old, married, father of three, had proven to be the perfect body guard for Boris Yeltsin with his even temper and quick wit. He literally looked up to his President, being four inches shorter.

"You both will be expected to remain in the area. We will be in touch on this phone assigned to you by the CIA."

Dimitri held up a cell phone, a new device for the two newest residents of Eagle Ridge. "This phone needs to be on your person, Denis, wherever you go. We will call daily with updates. You may monitor the news on television, but don't believe everything you hear. Mr. Jackson and I will provide you with what you need to know. The room went silent for a minute or two with Anotonov's last words. Yeltsin rose from the couch and walked to a sliding door located just off the kitchen. He had a pack of Russian cigarettes that he was beginning to open when Anotonov stopped him. "What, Dimitri. I can't smoke here?" "Mr. President, you may smoke anywhere you like, you just can't smoke that brand - if someone should see that pack." Yeltsin smiled and waved him off before he could complete his sentence. "I understand, my friend." Jackson pointed to several shopping bags that had been laid on the kitchen island. "There's enough food for one week, including a carton of cigarettes. Beyond that, you will shop at the local store down the hill. A car will be delivered here tomorrow." Jackson then reached out and took the foreign pack of cigarettes from the President.

The two officers kept the best for last, Boris and Denis's temporary identifications. Both men became more attentive as Anotonov continued. Boris sat remembering a time when he went by a nickname when he was younger, working his way up in the Communist Party. His fellow officer candidates called him: Bol'shaya sobaka or Big Dog. The name became so much a part of his personality that when someone in his family called him Boris he didn't always respond right away. One time his mother, at a family reunion, asked if he might be losing his hearing. They all had a good laugh when he gladly shared his nickname.

"Mr. President, you will be known as Yuri Blachenko, and Denis will be your brother Ivan. Your story: The two of you are traveling to various parts of the United States to see where you'd like to relocate family and some friends from eastern Europe. The less said the better. Do not go into much detail with any neighbors. We're not sure how long you will be here, hopefully not more than a few weeks. But it could be up to a couple of months. We just don't know at this point." Anotonov looked away and then continued.

"Mr. President, you asked about your wife earlier. She and two of your children and their families have been relocated to the Georgian countryside near the Black Sea. I received confirmation that they are there and safe. We will let them know you and Denis are out of harm's way, but no one is to know your location, is that clear?"

Boris looked first at Denis, who sat to his left, then stood and looked down on Dimitri and nodded. As the black SUV exited the driveway, Denis walked to the back sliding doors by the kitchen and pulled the drawstring, allowing the curtains to open. The doors faced east and the openness showcased the sun rising and a freshly mowed backyard.

"I like the shape of back area, Boris. A nice border fence and pleasant view of the hills beyond. We should consider going for walk and know more about the land."

§

Saturday mornings in Eagle Ridge were a welcomed sight for early risers, especially in the Spring. Jack made it a point to get the day started by taking a walk and getting a few thousand steps in before eight a.m. He had Dash on a leash, coffee in his free hand, as they made their way down and around Lincoln Boulevard. The view of the valley that ran northwest toward I-90 was breathtaking. As far as Jack was concerned, life at that moment in time felt great. Dash would stop occasionally and smell the roses, hydrants, trash cans, and various other landmarks that called to him as he did his business. This was really Dash's time to visit the spots that left some mark or message as Jack liked to think of it. "Who is it today, Dash? The Anderson's collie? Or that little poodle living behind us? Dash would look up, smile, then walk off shaking his collar as he went. This was their time. Ellen was sleeping in and her boys were getting some exercise out along the Parkway, which made her smile under her eye shade when she heard them leave. Jack and Dash gradually made their way back up Lincoln after strolling through the nearby quarry where Dash would drop a load, making the climb back up the hill a little easier.

Drinking his morning coffee and walking the dog was his morning exercise ritual, but it also served another purpose. Jack was checking on the "Hood," which was Jack's nickname for the Eagle Ridge Community he served as: Landscape Committee Chairman. He and Ed, his co-chair, led a small group that were charged by the HOA with keeping nearly five hundred community households in compliance with the standards set out by the organization they voluntarily served. Ed took the responsibility more seriously than Jack, but Jack was the chairman and, as Ellen reminded Jack often, keeping Eagle Ridge looking good was no joke. To Jack, everything in life was fair game when it came to jokes. Everything.

When Jack finished his coffee, he placed the container inside his backpack and reached for his small notepad and pen. Dash sniffed a fire hydrant, checking for another message, while Jack scribbled down a quick note concerning the paint that was beginning to peel on an entire block of community fence nearby. Jack stood making the notation - hands free. He'd attached Dash's leash to a carabiner on his backpack. *Ingenious*, Ellen offered when she'd walked with them the previous week. "That move you just made could come back to literally bite you in the ass if Dash alerted suddenly." Jack accepted the compliment and the suggestion with a smile. The arrangement only made sense to him, since he needed to make notes while they walked.

The dark orange colored community fence set the standard for the residents, and peeling paint definitely sent the wrong message to visitors and monthly dues payers. As Jack went to adjust his backpack, Dash quit walking briskly and froze, jerking Jack around, nearly sending him to the ground. Jack's pen and notepad went one way, while he spun like a top, yanking first to the left and then quickly to the right as Dash began to tug the leash and bark. Jack looked down the street, but to no avail, as he continued to spin. He needed to gather himself as he ordered Dash to STOP.

First, Jack adjusted his sunglasses and located his notepad and pen in the gutter near a puddle of muddy water. Thankfully, the pad rested on top of some debris, only slightly damaged. "Dash - settle down - please stop." The cute little canine finally quit barking, but continued to look across the street, tail wagging. "Strange," Jack whispered to himself. "What are you looking at?" Jack followed Dash's gaze and spotted two men, he did not recognize, who were coming the opposite direction on the other side of Lincoln. They both stopped when Dash began to bark.

Normally, people that were out early, before nine on Saturday morning, walked their dogs, ran sprints, or walked together at a quick pace. Jack noticed that these two were slowly strolling along before stopping, which made Jack a little suspicious. "Sorry, Dash, good boy," Jack stroked the dog as he continued to look at the men who had begun to move on.

Jack unwound Dash from his leg, feeling a little silly, but thankful that he'd spun in front of two strangers and not in front of Ellie Wilson, the wife of the HOA President. Ellie jogged regularly around Eagle Ridge as an unofficial greeter in the community she considered her own. To be honest, Jack always felt Ellie was performing compliance checks on the HOA codes and rules.

Jack picked up his pace, huffing and puffing as he made his way back to the house with a reluctant Dash close behind. Ellen greeted them when they entered. "You're back early. Don't tell me, Dash pooped again on Ramona's driveway." "Car keys," came Jack's breathless response. "What's the matter?" "I have to go, take Dash, unleash, got to go, strangers down the street." "Stop, Jack, and quit talking in code. Take a damn breath and tell me what's going on?"

Jack took a breath and looked at Ellen. "Dash alerted when he saw two strangers just a few minutes ago. Funny thing is, he acted like he knew the men or at least one of them – he kept wagging his tail." "Okay, go with your instinct. I've got Dash, go!"

The garage door barely cleared the roof of the Subaru as Jack exited in a hurry narrowly missing one of their bikes. He returned a few minutes later looking dejected and a little confused. "They may be visitors, because I could tell, they are not from around here," Jack nearly shouted. Ellen stood drinking coffee, surprised with the level of disappointment in Jack's voice. He was surprised by the fact that two big men, walking slowly, would vanish so quickly. "I'm confident of one thing El." "What's that?" "I could identify them if I had to, especially the one with the mustache."

Chapter 3

EAGLE RIDGE - SPOKANE, WASHINGTON

"Well, Denis, what do you think about this Eagle Ridge place?" The newest residents were experiencing their second morning on American soil and had finished their excursion around the immediate neighborhood, a walk of about a mile and a quarter. They stood inside by the backdoor slider of the place they would call home for who knows how long? "I think the area is very quiet, almost too quiet, sir. But it is wide open, especially in back area with nice views of the hills around." Boris lit his third cigarette of the morning and remarked at how mild the American brand tasted than what he, and most Russians, were used to smoking. Denis smiled and looked down at the floor and then back up at Boris. The Russian President could tell his bodyguard had something on his mind. Boris moved his hand holding the cigarette back and forth as a sign for Denis to speak. "That guy walking the dog – he must be new at dog walking." Denis could barely complete his thought before Boris burst out laughing. "Yes, comrade, his dog walking is funnier than this fake mustache I must wear – or is it?" Boris's comment caused both men to laugh once again as he moved the large hairy addition above his lip, back and forth in Charlie Chaplin fashion, one of his favorite comedic actors. Both men agreed that the laugh felt good, much like the walk they had just taken. Both exercises were most welcomed at this point in their extremely stressful lives.

The morning had started out brisk and both men wore light jackets as a result. Denis took Boris's jacket and hung it up in the front hall closet. Both jackets were new and had the Nike brand on them, but neither man recognized the famous label. All their clothes were new, which took a little getting used to, now that Boris was no longer required to wear a suit or Denis his uniform of bland shades of brown. Both especially enjoyed the blue jeans with the more flexible waist bands and the multi-colored long-sleeved shirts and sweaters. The t-shirt that Denis wore had the Nike slogan of *Just Do It* across the front. Denis pointed to the slogan on his shirt as he passed Boris on his way to the kitchen to make bacon and eggs for breakfast. Denis was not known to be humorous and Boris appreciated his attempt to keep things light.

Each man had their appointed duties. Boris busied himself by sitting at the kitchen counter with his writing tablet, making plans for creating a new government with his trusted associates. Vladimir Putin would be instrumental in administering government activities in Boris's absence. Yeltsin trusted Putin and believed him to be a worthy candidate for leadership in the future. All communication between the two men was understandably cut off, for security reasons, which was carefully monitored by Bernard Jackson and his team. Denis would keep watch for any suspicious behavior near the home and was to report any such behavior immediately to Jackson. The household duties would also be his responsibility. Boris joked that he might be assassinated while Denis was vacuuming and the trusted bodyguard wouldn't know, until he shut the machine off.

§

Jack sat at his office desk on the crisp March morning and opened his file on the West Plains Development. He had a caffeine buzz going and Steely Dan's "Reelin' in the Years" in his headset, which according to the mayor's office last directive, was not an acceptable activity. Jack reviewed and passed along a few of the directives coming from the man he referred to as: Mayor Blowhard, and dismissed the rest as he took another sip. He enjoyed going up against the man's authority, almost tempting the mayor, or his most trusted assistant, Fenton, to police their commandments. "Now there's a guy I'd keep an eye on," Jack would tell his colleagues' City Hall associates. "Fenton Benton? Who names a child in rhyme? No wonder the guy is an

associate of the mayor. You can smell the anger on the poor man."

Last year, Jack and Ed pulled a prank on Mr. Benton. According to the more relaxed, less anal, people who work at City Hall, the clever ruse played on the mayor's right-hand man will be remembered forever.

It happened almost a year ago to the day last March, Friday the eighth in the afternoon around 2:30pm. The day, unusually warm, with blue skies showcased early budding of flowers and leafy trees throughout Riverfront Park. From the office windows on the south and east sides of City Hall, the park along the river burst with Spring colors, right on cue.

It was the perfect time to visit, and Spokane was hosting Sister City representatives from County Cork, Ireland in a pre-Saint Patrick's Day celebration. The mayor unfortunately had a conflict, which prevented him from being able to host the day-long festivities organized by the Spokane's Sister City chair, Ms. Corrine Bundle. Standing in for the mayor and happily representing the City Government would be none other than Mr. Fenton Benton. Tall, lean, and bow-tied, he stood ready to represent the City of Spokane. Every department in City Hall had sent in their thoughts for participation on this special day – except one – the Planning Department. There was bad blood between the PD and Mr. Benton and almost everyone employed there knew it. Benton could not stand anyone in the Planning Department, starting with Jack. It seemed as though every time Mayor Walters's office attempted to push the PD to favor certain developers over others, the more push back they received from Jack. "It's all politics and I'm not going to play that game," Jack would tell Ed. The conflict caused Jack and Fenton to butt heads more than once, with Jack winning ultimate approvals through his wit and charm, two attributes that were sorely lacking in Mr. Benton's personality.

When Jack found out about the Sister City event, he envisioned an opportunity to take advantage of it, even if it meant losing his job. What began as a fun idea soon developed into a highly synchronized prank. In Jack's words, "One thing led to another, until the idea burst into a very real possibility."

After reading the list of festivities planned for the day, Jack noticed that the Riverfront Park Skyride, a unique round trip gondola ride over the falls, was a featured attraction. And why not? The Spokane Falls were especially beautiful that time of year, pouring large volumes of water over the falls from melting snows that covered peaks from miles around. The rushing water cascaded over huge outcrops and boulders that had been shaped and placed thousands of years ago by regional ice age floods. This uniquely beautiful and spectacular site cut through the heart of downtown Spokane within view of City Hall. The contingent from Ireland would be invited to ride over the falls, a thirty-minute ride that was worth every second of a visitor's time. The gondolas started in the park and passed between the Washington Water Power building and City Hall. The ride traveled along within the view of offices located on the northside of the City Hall building, including the Council Chambers where the event would take place. *Perfect*, Jack thought to himself as he completed his scheme and shared it with Ed and Jimmy.

"Let me get this straight, Jack. You want to send Fenton over the falls at the same time he is to give his keynote address to the city with the people from Ireland in attendance?

"In a gondola of course, Ed!" Jack had his head bent slightly to the left with hands out in front of him, laughing, while Ed just looked up at the ceiling, arms folded as if this was going to be their last prank before being demoted or fired. "Ah, come on, Ed. There's no nobody else that can pull this off but you and me – and Jimmy."

The three schemers were sitting in a small windowless office, used primarily for storing old desks and chairs. Jack stopped talking when Jimmy raised his hand. "Jimmy, you don't have to raise your hand, go ahead, what is it?" Jimmy put his hand down immediately. "What, what's *my* part in this?" Jimmy looked as though Jack had just asked him to shoot the mayor.

Jack explained Jimmy's role as being critical to the success of the whole idea. "You are to escort Benton to the skyride as, supposedly, a surprise for the Irish visitors." It would be a last-minute change that Benton should, but will not question – Jack hoped.

"That's key, Jimmy. You know how to sell, don't you? You worked at Starbucks, right?" Jimmy hesitated, at first, wondering where this was going, then after stares from both Jack and Ed, he remembered putting the manager's award for selling the most breakfast sandwiches one week on his resume. The fact that Jimmy ate most of those sandwiches was never mentioned, so he just smiled and nodded.

Jimmy enjoyed working with the two men and was grateful for his job at city hall. Evidently, becoming an accomplice, in this case learning to sell for real, was part of his job description. After all, Jack's the boss. "You have to really sell the last-minute change, got it, Jimmy? Ed and I are depending on you."

"Ah, yeah, sure Mr. Templeman, no, no problem."

The skeptic in Ed had doubts about Jack's plan. A lot depended on people reacting as Jack imagined they would. But Jack being Jack, who could charm a python if he had to, managed to convince Ed to help pull it off. Ed finally had to laugh at the idea. Patting Jack's shoulder as Jimmy showed a nervous smile, he declared, "You are the master of entertaining deceit, my friend."

The morning of the big day, even Jack had some doubts. He'd always thought the Sister City exchange was a waste of time, but he'd never felt closer to his Irish ancestry than he did at that moment. There were more important issues facing the city: crime, whether to add fluoride to the water, and what to do about the growing homeless problem, just to name a few. Jack had the plan playing out in a daydream streaming in his head when Jimmy interrupted. "Mr. T?" The greeting startled Jack, causing him to nearly spill the coffee cup he held. "Oh, sorry, Mr. T., didn't mean to…" "Jimmy. You… are you ready to do this?" "Ah, yes, sir. I just wanted to thank you for the opportunity, that's all, nothing more. Jack smiled, nodded his head and finished his coffee.

The visiting Irish contingent gathered together under the direction of Ms. Bundle, downstairs in the City Council Chambers. The eight members of the group consisted of four men and four ladies. The leader of the group, Sir Ian McKenna, had been looking forward to catching up with Mayor Walters. The two hit it off when the Spokane contingent visited Ireland two years earlier. When Jack found this out from Ms. Bundle earlier in the week, it made his day. Jack agreed to escort Mr. Fenton to the Chambers prior to the ceremony. It was just dumb luck that Ms. Bundle, in her motherly manner, set Jack up with Fenton. She figured the two men needed to find a way to resolve their differences, so Jack, becoming part of the ceremony, made sense to her. Jack's plan was coming together!

"Okay, Jimmy, let's go." The two headed out the door, Jack upstairs to the mayor's office and Jimmy to meet Ed on the second-floor skywalk.

When Jack walked into the mayor's office he could hear Fenton in the background. "Ms. Martin, I need that final comment page for my speech, NOW." Benton's secretary rushed past Jack heading for the printer. "Hey, Shelly, having a good day?" Shelly almost tripped as she attempted to answer Jack. "Oh, hi, Jack. He's in the mayor's office." Jack smiled, shook his head and moved toward his mark. When the flustered assistant to Mayor Walters saw Jack coming through the door, Benton instinctively grabbed his desk phone and raised it to his ear, faking a call. Jack knew the ruse, played it on associates as a joke, more than once himself. "You ready, Fenton?"

"Ah, yes, Templeman, just a minute. Shelly's getting something for me." The phone fell from his shoulder to the desk, and then to the floor. Fenton didn't seem to notice. Jack continued to stand in the doorway, waiting for the idiot, like a lion surveying his prey. Jack patiently watched Benton fumble through a file for no apparent reason. Jack held his smile for as long as it took. "You're making this too easy, Fenton." The man looked back at Jack. "What'd you say?" "Nothing. You ready?"

Ed met Jimmy on the skywalk holding an Irish flag on a three-foot pole. "You know what to do, Jimmy. Make us proud." The young intern nodded and took off for the back entrance of the City Council Chambers.

"Okay, Templeman, I'm ready." The tall lanky Mayoral substitute donned a green jacket, purchased just for this occasion, and proceeded to straighten his arms to make sure the cuffs of his shirt were exactly one inch below the sleeve of the new jacket. Benton looked in a mirror as he passed by, stopped for a second to straighten his tie, then turned and brushed past Jack through the door. As they headed for the elevators Jack spoke up. "Ah, there's a slight change of plans, Fenton." "Change?" Fenton pursed his lips and scrunched his eyebrows as he spoke.

Jack returned the look as he replied, "Yes, we need to meet one of my associates at the backdoor of the Chambers."

"What, why?" Fenton relaxed his look, but did his best in questioning Jack.

"Corrine wants you to surprise our visitors before your welcoming speech."

"Surprise, I hate surprises."

"Yeah, I know…I mean, I do too, but, hey, it's the mayor's idea." Jack could see beads of sweat beginning to form on his mark's forehead.

"Well, if the mayor…" Reluctantly, Fenton Benton agreed.

The two men walked around to the backdoor where Jimmy stood holding the Irish flag. Jack began to say something when Benton interrupted. "Don't tell me, this kid waves the flag as I give my speech?" "Close, but no. Jimmy is going to escort you to the Skyride where you will enter the lead gondola with the flag, ahead of the Irish, who will be boarding behind you." "That doesn't make sense, Templeman." "I know, right? But that's what Ms. Bundle and Mayor Walters are expecting, and we don't have much time to make this happen… sir."

Sweat began to run into Fenton's eyes as he returned Jack's *what's the matter?* look. He began to reflexively blink, one eye then the other, finally nodded and went with Jimmy across the street and into the adjoining park area, wiping his eyes on his perfect green sleeve as he went. They disappeared for a few seconds as Jack quickly ascended the back stairway to the floor above the skywalk.

The purple-colored gondolas hung waiting for the man with the Irish flag, like co-conspirators ready to join in the fun. Ed linked up with Jack and the two traded off watching as the gondola operator opened the door for Fenton to enter the ride. "Whew." Both men looked at one another and sighed. Ed taped Jack on the arm and pointed toward the gondolas. Jack looked again through the binoculars. He found Jimmy, looking back at Jack, waving frantically, smiling and dancing, as if he'd just pulled off the biggest heist in history. "No, no, Jimmy, stop!" The boy kept going until he saw Jack and Ed signaling him to stop, immediately. Just then, Fenton's gondola began its descent down toward the falls. It was a beautiful day as Fenton Benton, representing Mayor Ira Walters, looked around in time to see Jimmy finish his dancing with a wave toward City Hall. Fenton looked back in the same direction and saw Jack hand the binoculars to Ed. *Templeman!* With fury in his eyes, Fenton turned to yell at his escort, but Jimmy was nowhere in sight. Instead, Jimmy and the gondola operator were behind a pillar discussing how the system worked, a clever ruse devised by Jack in case Fenton wanted to stop the ride.

Ed and Jack took off, running toward the Council Chambers. Fenton Benton, now locked securely inside the purple gondola, headed for the scenic Spokane Falls and into the rainbow-colored mist that rose to greet him – instead of entering the Council Chambers. The gondola gently swayed as the mist wrapped around the windows of the bright purple capsule. It's normally a thrilling ride, but Mr. Benton was no longer in the mood to carry out what he thought was the mayor's change in plans. He sat defeated and angry, knowing Jack Templeman duped him one again.

In the meantime, Jack and Ed entered the Chambers where Corrine Bundle and fifty guests, the Irish visitors, three television reporters and their crews, other media and a small catering staff from the Davenport Hotel were gathered. The Irish visitors and several business leaders stood talking, waiting to be seated before hearing Mr. Benton's welcoming speech, which would not take place because he happened to be sitting alone on a Skyride gondola, dejectedly holding an Irish flag. "Where's Fenton? Ms. Bundle whispered to Jack as he approached her. "Corrine, there's been a slight change of plans."

Jack explained that Fenton thought it would be more exciting to welcome the Irish from the gondola rather than to give a speech. The normally calm matron of City Hall reached for her perfumed hankie and proceeded to dab it across her forehead. "The man must be off his nut, Jack." Corrine whispered as she continued dabbing. "What are we to do?" Jack went from standing beside her to standing in front of her and suggested, right on time, that everyone look out the large picture window and wave to Mr. Benton as he passed by. Fenton looked up just in time to see Ms. Bundle waving her hankie. Jack looked over her shoulder, wishing silently that he had been videotaping the moment. The disgruntled government employee decided to make the most of a bad situation and began waving the Irish flag as the purple gondola disappeared into the watery mist of the falls.

Ms. Bundle looked at Jack, shook her head, then, after taking a deep breath, asked everyone to sit. She then turned the meeting over to Jack who graciously agreed to read

Mayor Walters's address, laced with a few jokes of course.

§

Boris and his sidekick, Denis, watched as a blue sedan entered the driveway. This would be their transportation during their stay. The Russians and Americans in charge decided that it would look suspicious if the men didn't have a car. Boris looked out the front door after the driver handed him the keys to a Volvo. "A Volvo, not bad," Denis confirmed as he finished cooking sausage and onion omelets.

"Yes, I agree, my friend. We could have ended up with Jeep or, God forbid, a Russian made vehicle." They both burst out laughing. Each enjoyed the idea that they had a ride of their own. They would be followed wherever they went, of course, but it felt good to know they would be the lead car.

After a few days being housebound, the two displaced Russians decided to take a drive. Denis was thankful that they weren't relocated to Great Britain. "I hate driving on wrong side of road." Boris didn't skip a beat; "It would have been more fun if our families could have joined us and we were sent to Caribbean or Hawaii." More laughter as the two headed downtown to check out the Falls they'd heard about. "We are becoming tourists, Denis." Tourists with chaperones," Boris shared with the man he most trusted with his life.

They parked the car, as did their chaperones, at parking meters outside City Hall. The center of Spokane's government - located on the bank of the Spokane River at the Falls. Jack always considered it to be the most wasted real estate downtown. "This whole building should be broken up into condos with retail on the main floor," Jack would tell anyone who asked.

The two Russians were impressed with the location and decided to walk along Post Street to the bridge of the same name. Looking down they watched as the rushing water cascaded onto huge boulders, causing a strong mist to rise up and greet them intermittently. The Monroe Street bridge directly downstream from them had people receiving the same attention from the river below. "You know, Denis, if we stand here long enough, we won't have to take showers."

Boris had to adjust his mustache, which had begun to slip because of the wetness. They walked back over the bridge, reversing their direction and into Riverfront Park. Denis remarked about how much this place reminded him of another in Russia when Boris stopped him. "You see that big tent-like structure by the building with painted horses going around and around?" Denis nodded his head and listened as Boris explained how Spokane had a World's Fair that Russia participated in back in 1974. "That structure was the U.S. pavilion, Russia's pavilion was somewhere over there." He pointed to an area not far from where they stood. "So, you see that Russia and Spokane have history." They proceeded to walk a little further before Boris stopped once again by pushing his hand into Denis's chest. "That man over there. He is same man we saw walking dog in Eagle Ridge." Denis looked and agreed. "Yes, the one that did that silly dance with his dog, that's him alright. He must work near here," Denis suggested. Was this a coincidence or fate? Boris could not get over the odd chance that this would happen. Boris and Denis continued their walk along the river as Jack met Ellen for lunch by the carousel on Spokane Falls Blvd.

§

Jack enjoyed remembering the Irish incident so much he pulled a file he'd put together recapping the fallout. Corrine Bundle provided insightful notes regarding the mayor's response upon his return. The short report began with the mayor's rant. The file: 00033462: **IRISH VISIT.**

"No, no, no, NO! That Jack Templeman is going to be the death of me yet," Walters shouted after learning about the Sister City fiasco. The mayor's vocal outbreak included a series of mumbled words that nobody could understand. Shelly, his dedicated secretary, stood frozen in the mayor's doorway as he hung up his phone, slammed back into the receiver to be exact. After working nearly thirty years at City Hall, which included serving four Mayors, she knew something had to be done about Jack Templeman and told Mayor Walters so. Shelly M.

Shelly and Ira were about the same age, single, workaholics, dedicated to making Spokane a great city. They just had different ways of expressing their emotions. For that reason, Shelly felt that they had a special bond. Her loyalty meant a great deal to the mayor. And her soothing comments calmed the situation, as they did in previous situations, at least for the moment.

Mayor Walters was through with Jack's shenanigans. There were some pranks that he couldn't prove, like the time his portrait in the lobby had Mickey Mouse ears added, or the free taco night where the mild and the extra hot sauce signs were switched. The list went on and on. Years of having to put up with Jack's jokes and sarcasm, at inappropriate times, had finally run their course as far as the mayor was concerned.

Mr. Benton requested, and received, a leave of absence. He now suffered from recurring nightmares and headaches that caused him to lose sleep and eat less. At six feet tall and weighing in at just under one hundred and forty pounds, serving in a high-stress job, he could afford neither.

Fenton could not stop visualizing the embarrassing ride over the Falls that fateful day. The next day, when he arrived at work, and looked up at the beautifully rejuvenated, former Montgomery Ward store, now gracing downtown as City

Hall, the nightmare replayed in his head. All Fenton could envision was Corrine Bundle pressing both hands against the City Council room window, watching, as he disappeared over the Falls into the mist, instead of standing in for the mayor at the podium. Fenton had been fooled, yet again, and it didn't feel good on him, again.

Even his cat, Margie, named after his favorite aunt, who willed the oversized feline on to him after she passed away last year, couldn't console the poor man. His desperate hope, which slowly waned as he ate his normal breakfast of shredded wheat, jellied toast and a poached egg, was that the mayor would figure out some means of punishment for those who conspired against him, the hopeful future Mayor of Spokane. That too was part of the diminishing hope and dream of this man who lived a few blocks away from City Hall, along the Spokane River, down in Peaceful Valley.

From his kitchen window, he could see the Falls of the river. The mist rising as the water cascaded through the canyon, surrounding the river, to land close by with an accompanying roar. He respected the power of the Falls, he kept telling himself, as he wiped some milk from the side of his mouth. He used to enjoy riding the Skyride over the roiling water, especially that time of year. Maybe that was it! If he kept thinking positively about the Falls, he might come out of his depressed state and feel better about himself.

Benton decided that he would do just that. And, so he did. He even said it out loud, causing the cat to waddle off and hide. "I like the Falls and I will do my job, in spite of those who consider City Hall a comedy club."

Two days later, after five days of being on leave, Fenton was back on the job. The man smiled as he re-entered City Hall, walked past Ernie, the guard, who made him stop and re-enter the metal detector after forgetting to remove his keys. Fenton apologized, took a deep breath, and pushed the elevator button for the sixth floor. Ernie watched and shook his head as the door closed on Fenton Benton. Fenton felt like a new man. He and the Mayor had some catching up to do and Fenton looked forward to every minute.

§

The doorbell rang at Boris and Denis's new residence. Boris lay snoring on the couch in the family room as Denis walked to the front door with his right hand at his back holding his MP443 Grach handgun steady. He checked for shadows in the glassine relight – there was one, small unmoving. Turning slightly to his left, Denis looked out the eyehole to see a matronly lady holding a pie. She looked up and smiled knowing what the eyeball meant on the other side peephole.

Denis replaced the gun in his waistband at the small of his back, quickly checked himself in the hallway mirror before opening the door.

"You must be the new homeowner," came a high-pitched sweet voice. I'm Amy Brewster, we, my husband Fred and I, live across the street. The lady pointed back over her shoulder with her free hand as she spoke. We, that is I, would like to welcome you to the neighborhood. Fred would be here but he, unfortunately, stepped in some tree sap on the way over and had to hobble home to clean his boot." Amy waited for Denis to comment, but he said nothing. Amy and Denis were in a stare down until he realized he should introduce himself. "Oh, excuse please, Mrs. Brewster, I'm Ivan, Ivan

Blachenko." They shook hands, causing Amy to test her ability to balance a pie with one hand.

Amy continued, "I couldn't wait for Fred, he'll probably be all day with that sap, and the French Apple pie couldn't wait either." With that said, Amy thrust the warm pie into the waiting hands of her new neighbor. Denis accepted the baked dessert with a big toothy smile that was beginning to hurt his face. "Thank you. You are very kind Mrs. Brewster." The little lady giggled as he said her name. "Oh, you have an accent. Let me guess: German? No. Dutch? We have Dutch relatives, but you need to talk more before I'd really know for sure if you're one of them. Ah, the pie is French Apple. I know you're not French. You're not, right?"

"No, I'm neither French nor Dutch, Mrs. Brewster. I am Russian." "Oh, my, we, that is I, don't know any people from Russia, but your people are certainly in the news lately." Denis nearly dropped the pie when Amy made the comment about the news. She stepped back a step after handing the pie over to Denis and asked if he knew the Miller family who lived there before? Denis didn't want to say too much in that moment, standing, smiling, holding a pie. A few seconds went by before he asked Mrs. Brewster if she didn't mind, but he wanted to try some of the pie before it cooled down. "Oh, my, yes, of course. Go." She nodded and started walking away. No sooner had Denis begun to do the, unrehearsed, smiling door closing ritual, when, out of the corner of his eye he saw Boris come up alongside him.

The President had been taking a nap in the other room and stood yawning by the time he reached the door. Denis looked at Boris with a desperate expression. "What is it my friend, or should I say, who is at door?" The reason Denis cringed was that Boris had forgotten to apply his fake mustache. Amy noticed the new arrival and proceeded back toward the door.

"Oh, hello, I'm Amy, Amy Brewster from across the street, over there." As Mrs. Brewster turned and pointed, Denis did the same into the hall mirror. Boris slapped his hand to his face immediately, not knowing what else to do. With a covered hand over his mouth, he introduced himself, but neither Amy or Denis could understand a word. "That's my brother, Yuri, Denis declared. Boris bowed as he excused himself.

Mrs. Brewster noticed the quick exit and adjusted her footing on the porch. She stepped back and down a step and with a slight smile and turning her head slightly said: "He must be very shy. Is he Russian too? A brother you say? You two don't look alike." Her voice trailed off as Denis smiled and nodded, re-engaging the ritual, slowly, slowly closing the door.

§

What Amy Brewster and the other neighbors didn't know was that their neighborhood harbored an international fugitive, and his bodyguard. The very man who went from being the heralded President of Russia after the dissolution of the USSR to become hunted by his communist opposition. He wasn't just any political runaway hiding from harm, but Boris Yeltsin, a leader who promised a new way of life for all Russians. His economic initiatives were not currently working as planned, causing problems within the Communist Party, especially his opposition. Yeltsin's absence appears to be necessary to some of his people and irresponsible to others who wanted him to stand and fight. His opposition saw this time as an opportunity to hunt him down and eliminate the problem. The media around the world couldn't have been more pleased. The disappearance of President Yeltsin had become the biggest news of the day from two perspectives: 1. Where is He? and 2. Why did he leave? The second perspective gave Yeltsin's opposition the hype they needed and the media couldn't get enough of the dirt, even if it wasn't totally accurate. The big question for everyone involved in the clandestine operation was: How long would this story continue?

The white Chevrolet Suburban that stopped by the newly occupied residence in Eagle Ridge didn't seem out of place. In fact, it matched a few of the soccer mom Suburbans that actually belonged in the area. It wasn't until the Suburban stopped and the men in dark glasses stepped out that someone might have considered the moment a little odd. The patrolling unit, government jargon, performed scheduled sweeps at various intervals, would occur twenty-four hours a day, seven days a week while Yeltsin remained in the United States.

Two hours went by with Boris and Denis meeting with Bernard Jackson and one member of his team in the living room. The residence had been outfitted at the last minute with second hand furnishings and it was up to Jackson to keep Boris comfortable. "It's not the Presidential Palace, but given the circumstances Mr. Jackson, we're fine here."

The style could be considered casual contemporary. The couch had some worn spots, and the chairs sagged a little. The house had been professionally cleaned. The white walls, adorned with a few landscape prints, helped to make the place look normal. The wall-to-wall, tan colored carpeting looked relatively new and a fake Ficus tree stood seven feet high in one of the corners. Jackson's driver stood guard inside at the back slider, the third man in this visiting entourage.

Boris was given an update on his family and his administration's status by the woman to Jackson's right. His followers were reportedly laying low as he had directed them to do, through another trusted aid, Mikhail Gorbachev. "The bottom line is that you may need to stay here for at least another two weeks," Jackson stated with authority. "I'm not sure I can do that, comrade," came Yeltsin's response. "It's for your own good as well that of your family. "Mr. President, this is the only way we can ensure your safety."

Yeltsin knew that people, most of whom he didn't know, were putting their own lives on the line for him and he deeply appreciated their commitment to save his life and the lives of his family and followers. "Give me the moment, Mr. Jackson, I need to think. Actually, I need to pee, which also helps me to think."

Jackson told Yeltsin to take his time and that they'd be in touch. "The fact is, Mr. President, you have no other choice at this time, but to sequester here in Spokane. We want you to stay close to this residence. Denis can leave, but you need to stay here, is that clear?" The comment didn't sit well with Boris or his bodyguard. Denis looked at Jackson with disdain. Everyone close to Boris Yeltsin knew the man didn't like to be told what to do. After the government people left, Denis watched as the man he guarded with his life headed for the bathroom. Boris flicked on the light and fan and slammed the door. "We'll be fine, sir, " shouted Denis.

After a few minutes, Boris returned. He looked over at Denis and smiled, puffed out his chest and spoke in a soft tone, "It's okay if we take to walking around this place, if we remain on sidewalks and pathways, correct?" Denis nodded. "We also have a car and have traveled to the store and downtown without a problem." Denis agreed. "I think we are safe, Denis, in this place – Spokane."

Denis made his way around the couch and sat next to Boris. "Sir, you are always safe with me. Your family is being taken care of, and, right now, we are going to have lunch! Ham sandwiches and French apple pie." Boris looked at the man sitting next to him, nodded his head, and put a hand on Denis's shoulder. "I have only one thing to add, comrade." "What is it sir?" "I have to pee, again."

§

Jack enjoyed creating new ideas at home, working on comedy routines with opening lines that led to twenty to thirty minutes of laughable banter. That's the best way to craft an act. At least, that's what he'd read in Steve Martin's interview in *Esquire Magazine*. He sat at the kitchen island. Capturing what came to mind and organizing it into a rhythm that would generate laughter, must be similar to writing a song and having it play in the media. So, fulfilling, unlike his work at City Hall. Inventing comedy brought him out of his workday rut. He prided himself on being able to think the opposite of what is expected. It sounded crazy to others when Jack tried to explain it, but it made perfect sense to him.

He read the newspaper, watched television and visited with Ellen as he wrote. The news media wound up being one of his greatest sources of comedy. The old saying; *You can't make this stuff up*, was never more telling than on television's nightly news cast.

Ellen busied herself at the kitchen stove, stirring a wok full of vegetables. The television news had just switched from local to national.

"Thank goodness, Spokane's news can be so boring at times," Jack offered as Ellen continued with dinner preparations.

"Oh, Jack, you don't think that a low crime rate isn't news?"

"Not especially. To me it just proves that even the criminals are bored."

"Now that's funny, Jack."

Topping the world news that particular night was the disappearance of Boris Yeltsin. As Jack put his notes away in his office, preparing to set the table for dinner, he noticed something odd. Dash, that wiry loveable mutt, went on alert and then walked slowly toward the television. The screen showed a video clip of Yeltsin standing on a tank giving a speech in Russia. "He's disappeared, and no one seems to know where in the world Boris Yeltsin is hiding," the commentator exclaimed.

The story didn't last that long, but Jack tapped Ellen on the shoulder and asked her to look at Dash. "What? He watches television with me sometimes. Especially ER with that young hunk, George Clooney." As soon as the news changed, Dash turned and barked. It was his time to eat too. Jack went to the laundry room to fill Dash's dish and make sure he had fresh water.

Ellen turned off the television and turned on some mellow dinner music. Dinner was served. Jack unfolded his napkin and looked at Ellen. "This meal smells terrific, El." He took a first bite and made an ugly face. "What, Jack?" He looked at her and grinned, "Just kidding, it's wonderful."

Mumbling through semi-spicy beans, meat and sauce, Jack continued. "So, Dash likes to watch news and ER, right?" Ellen looked at him before taking her next bite. "What's your point?" Jack looked up, took a quick drink of water, wiped his mouth and replied, "I just hope when Dash grows up, he'll consider becoming a doctor, not a news reporter." Ellen lifted her spoon and smiling, uttered, "Eat, Jacko."

# Chapter 4

## RIVERPARK SQUARE - SPOKANE, WA

Ed and Jack were having lunch in a new bistro downtown at Riverpark Square. "You know, Ed, I'm a little worried."

"About, what?"

"Sleepy's office. They haven't come up with any event or odd regulation that would make good material. That Irish Sister City event was the best." Ed nodded his head in agreement, then offered, "I agree. You'd think the mayor would have done something ridiculous by now." Ed had been secretly pleased with the fact that there hadn't been much push back from the Irish debacle.

A few bites later, Ed changed the subject. "So, how's your comedy act coming?" Jack explained that he had about 30 minutes of jokes that he felt good about. He wanted additional material that would have more of a national focus. "Watch more nightly news, Jack, it's full of material."

Jack waited a second before responding, "Maybe I should consult with Dash. Turns out he watches more television news than I do." Ed looked at his friend and laughed. Jack went on to explain how he feels about "life imitating art." And quickly followed up with the fact that he didn't mean Art Linkletter or Art Garfunkel. Ed laughed as did the older man sitting at the table next to them. "Hey, that's a good one, young man – you ought to be a comedian."

Before they left, Jack also mentioned the two men he saw last week walking in his neighborhood and how Dash alerted. Ed listened as Jack recounted the incident. "A strange situation, Ed. Let's just say I had an odd vibe off those two, and I think Dash picked up on it."

§

## MOSCOW, RUSSIA - ONE DAY AFTER YELTSIN'S ESCAPE

Col. Sergey Baskin, a trusted Yeltsin military officer, sat with his back to the windowless delivery van's wall, hands tied securely behind his back. *The driver must be crazy*, he thought as he attempted to see out of the dark hood that had been placed over his head. *What was happening?* He heard people shouting outside as the van maneuvered through traffic and over deep potholes. Most of the shouting appeared to support the man he'd protected just the day before – Boris Yeltsin. Someone next to Sergey asked where they were going. "Silence!" came a response accompanied by a few jabs from the butt of a rifle.

After what seemed like hours, the van passed through a

security gate then stopped after backing up. Doors opened, Sergey and two others were pulled from their sitting positions and forced onto a hard concrete surface face down. Someone behind him yanked the Colonel's arms up, causing great pain in his neck and shoulders as he managed to stand as ordered. Hoods were removed. Sergey found himself in the company of five of his men, who were in the process of having their heads shaved and pictures taken. Two guards holding AK-47s stood close by, rifles pointed in their captives' direction.

"Welcome to Lubyanka Prison. An institution you have helped to populate over the years, Colonel Baskin."

The voice came from behind. The familiar deep and stern voice of Colonel Rutskoy, a person he knew all too well. Rutskoy admitted to being in opposition to the cause that Yeltsin, and others, had been attempting to weave into a new existence for all Russian citizens. Unfortunately, democratic thinking didn't go over well with Alexander Rutskoy or most of the other communists involved in chasing Yeltsin from his homeland. *May God bless and protect our leader*, Sergey thought as he and the others were taken away.

The purging of key military followers loyal to Boris Yeltsin was nearly complete. Most of the high-ranking officials were safely under guard in prison. Those that remained at large, continued to guard the Presidential Palace, attempting to put down the coup that, currently, surrounded Moscow like a noose being tightened around a prisoner's neck.

Rutskoy and Putin met to finalize plans to find Yeltsin. "We need to bring this inept traitor back to be tried in a court of law," Putin shouted. "Find him. Do what you have to do, but find Yeltsin, Colonel!"

Torture was one of the more familiar ways of convincing people, under guard, to change their allegiance. And after a few hours, one of Yeltsin's support staff did just that. After a few bruises, broken bones and threats to kill his wife and children, Luka, Yeltsin's personal assistant, gave in. He'd overheard the relocation plan being discussed by an American as Yeltsin was swiftly transported out of his residence. Although the final destination was not revealed, people's names, those who were involved, were revealed. They would be tracked down and interrogated promptly. It was just a matter of time before Yeltsin would be coming home, in shackles and handcuffs. The other alternative was suicide, finding the poor, mentally unstable, drunken fool dead.

Chapter 5

Ed shared something that had been gnawing on him for about a week. He and Janice just returned from a short trip to the Oregon Coast at a cool little B&B they'd discovered last year after the Irish Sister City event. This year, he wanted to escape the ongoing chaos of City Hall, before the City Council voided Ed's two weeks, which was up for consideration, along with others, because of a budget shortfall. Tension levels were on the upswing at the office and Janice wanted to see relatives in Portland on the way down the coast. So, off they went. "Jack, look at me this is important," Ed asserted with a wrinkled forehead and brows crushed together. Jack looked at him and countered with, "Spill it, Ed."

Evidently, Janice spotted the two men Jack referred to a few days earlier. They were out walking through Whispering Pines Park. "We were loaded up, and on our way, but something told me to follow them, so we did." Ed stopped and took a sip of his usual Mayan Mocha latte before proceeding further. Jack waited a few beats then looked at Ed. "Well?"

"We knew the Miller place had people working on the yard and the house, Jack. Now we know why, those two moved into the Miller place. We saw them walk through the front door."

"What? Really? Hmm, interesting." Jack fell into thought. Ed watched as his friend's face slowly twisted, brows scrunched together, and eyes narrowed into that all too familiar thought look. The one that usually meant he was coming up with a subdivision name or a scheme of some kind. "Jack? What's going on in that head of yours?" Jack looked up. "Two guys? Suddenly appear out of nowhere, right, Ed?" Ed nodded his head, following along with Jack as he continued to slowly turn the wheels in his head. "I don't even remember an open house. How long has the Miller place been vacant? Six, maybe eight months?" Again, Ed nodded, "Yes. Their home went on the market late summer, but the price was too high and by the time they adjusted, bam, winter hit - a hard time to sell in Spokane."

They both sat there for a few moments looking at one another. Jack broke the silence. "We have to do something. We have to find out who these people are, Ed."

"Jacko, are we talking night vision goggles and camo gear at midnight or walking over and ringing the doorbell? Because one is very different from the other." Jack knew Ed was kidding about sneaking around in the dark. They'd only done that one time before, under a full moon on Halloween, to scare their wives two years ago. The four were playing cards at Ed and Janice's house, taking turns handing out candy at their front door. Since neither couple had children, they decided to make it a game night.

It was getting late, about 9:30, almost time to shut the porch lights off as the evening wound down. Ed excused himself from the table to go to the bathroom. On cue, Jack supposedly heard a noise outside and went out the back door to investigate, against the wishes of Janice and Ellen who sat looking at their cards. A few seconds later the doorbell rang. Both ladies looked at one another. Janice could hear the fan in the bathroom, and believing Ed was in there doing his thing, said that she'd get the door, thinking it was kids out late, probably teens. Ellen heard Janice talking and handing out candy, so she put her cards down and walked over to the front door. Four teens, dressed in drag, were just leaving. Janice closed the door, laughing at what she just witnessed. She walked to the bathroom, knocked on the door. "Ed, wrap it up, we're getting bored."

The doorbell rang again. Ellen was closest, having just put the bowl of candy down. She picked it back up, turned the knob and opened the door as Janice joined her. What they saw caused them both to scream in unison as they slammed the door shut and locked it.

Jack and Ed stood looking at one another through night vision goggles, giving each other a high five. They were dressed in full camo gear, black faces and holding a sign that read: "Trick or Treat, Ladies."

The evening went better, once the ladies decided to let them in after hearing familiar laughter emanating from outside the front door. Later that night, when the neighborhood lights went completely dark, it was time for the women to surprise the men, each in their respective homes. As it turned out, both wives liked their men in uniform, albeit a disguise. *Best Halloween ever!*

Finding out who the men were down the street was going to require some planning, but one thing was for sure, Jack and Ed were bound and determined to discover the identities of their new neighbors.

After contemplating his options, Jack decided, discretion being the very best part of valor, walking over to the new neighbors' residence and ringing the doorbell had to be the best option. After a drive-by earlier this week, he'd noticed some landscaping issues in their front yard that should be addressed. Perfect. So, armed with his Landscaping Rules and HOA Code Restrictions Sheets, Jack left the house on Saturday afternoon accompanied by Dash on his retractable leash. In spite of making numerous visits in the last year, fulfilling his voluntary duty and, simultaneously, getting to know the neighbors, he felt unusually nervous. Dash had just completed pooping on the new neighbor's front lawn. "Nice one, Dash," Jack said sarcastically as he filled the plastic bag. This was not the way he wanted to make an appearance as a landscape enforcer – holding a live doggie bag. As Jack completed cleaning up Dash's deposit, he noticed a man standing at the front window. Jack smiled and waved, the man nodded and slipped back into the shadow of the room. "That's odd," Jack whispered to Dash, who looked back at him, tail wagging. Undaunted, he reigned Dash in as they approached the front door. The man he'd noticed opened the door before Jack could ring the bell.

"Ah, hello there, I'm Jack Templeman, a neighbor and landscape committee chair for Eagle Ridge." Denis didn't say a word at first, just looked Jack up and down then said: "I like your dog." Jack felt a great weight of concern leave his shoulders and responded. "He's a Westie." Jack, trying not to sound awkward even though both men just stood staring at one another, went into his elevator speech about the importance of staying in compliance with the rules and regulations outlined in the sheets he pulled from a clipboard.

As the short conversion came to a conclusion, another man walked by in the hallway. The shortened leash suddenly tightened as Dash began to run toward the stranger in the background. Jack released the tension on the leash so the dog wouldn't hurt himself, resulting in Dash bolting through the front door past Denis and out of sight. Jack, without his knowing, had not secured the lock on the leash, which gave Dash approximately 40 feet of slack line. Denis ran into the house as Jack made several attempts to lock the leash while balancing the poop bag on top of the clipboard. That's when he heard Dash bark. There was confusion coming from inside the men's home – and then laughter. Next came a booming voice in a Russian accent, "Help. Help me. I'm being attacked by a white ball of fur!"

Jack stood holding the front door open, while doing his balancing act, calling for Dash. The line on the leash went slack as Denis came back holding Dash. The dog had a look of surprise on his face as if he'd never seen Jack before in his life. "I think you can reel this fish back in, Mr. Templeman." Jack put the clipboard and the poop bag down on the porch as Denis handed off the dog. The stocky man smiled and petted Dash, as his owner kept making excuses. "He normally doesn't do this. I'm so sorry, I hope he didn't disturb anything inside. Please let me know…" Jack suddenly stopped talking when the other man came around the corner and greeted his visitors with a big smile.

"You make the day, sir." Jack could tell by their accents that these men were from a country he'd never visited. The big guy with the mustache introduced them. "I'm Yuri Blachenko and this is brother to me, Ivan." Jack shook their hands, which felt more like muscular pillows, introducing himself to Yuri as Dash licked Yuri's hands he continued to scratch Dash under the chin. Both men seemed friendly enough, which gave Jack more relief, as the bigger man took a turn holding Dash.

Dash looked smaller, but very comfortable, in Boris's arms. The big man carefully put Dash on the floor as Jack said his goodbyes. "Sometimes taking Dash for a walk is like playing chess. I put him down, he moves, then I make a move to counter his move and so on." Jack made the comment because that's the way he felt at times. Dash was quick, but Jack had to be quicker. The two men looked at each other, then the older brother offered with a slight smile:

"Jack, you play chess?"

# *Chapter 6*

## TEMPLEMAN'S HOME - EAGLE RIDGE

Jack entered the house to the sounds of Ellen working out with Jane Fonda leading the way on television in the living room. He patted Dash on the head, unsnapped his leash, held the little dog's jaw in his hand, looked him straight in the eyes and told him what a good boy he'd been on their walk. It never failed to amuse Jack to witness the number of stops it took to go less than a mile around Whispering Pines Park and back. "Only fifteen stops this time," Jack announced to the house, the wind, Ellen, whoever was listening.

Dash took the patting in stride, but what he really wanted was a treat, which Jack, traditionally, rewarded the little guy from the familiar, green Goodies Galore box with several breeds of dogs adorning the front. Dash waited patiently as Jack fumbled to open the new box of multi-colored wafers. The canine watched, licked a paw, wagged his tail, and, as if almost impatiently, finally growled, as if to say; *Let me do it myself for God's sake.*

Jack made his way into the kitchen, adjacent to the living room. Dash followed with a treat safely tucked away in his mouth. "Honey, I'm back," Jack shouted over the loud instructions being hurled by Jane toward Ellen. "Not now, Jack, Jane and I are beginning to bond, finally." Ellen, dressed in leotards, sports bra, tank top and headband, matched her instructor, who counted backward from ten, performing a scissor kick.

"You'll never guess who's invited me to play chess with him." Ellen paused the video, gathered her breath, and stopped to listen. "Who, did what, Jack?" "One of the brothers that just moved into the Miller's place, asked me to play chess sometime."

The workout video ended a few minutes later and Ellen toweled off as Jack recounted his time with the new guys down the block. "It was Dash who made the whole thing happen. He bolted into the house when he saw Yuri." "Wait a minute, these guys are brothers? The two men you saw last week for the first time?" "Yes, Yuri and Ivan." Ellen made her way into the kitchen with the towel draped over her shoulder and water bottle in hand. "Hey, I didn't mean to interrupt." "Oh, not a problem, Jacko. I'd been with Miss Fonda long enough."

Ellen wanted to hear more about the two brothers. Jack told her that he was invited to stop by Monday night for dinner. "We're going to have a chess match." "You haven't had the chess board out in years, Jack, are you sure you're up for playing a Russian?" Ellen rolled her R's as she imitated a Russian accent. Jack added that he looked forward to finding out more about the two men, first, the chess match came second. "Besides, there are some landscaping compliance issues that also need to be addressed." Ellen stopped and turned as she headed for the shower adding, "So, there's no need for blackened faces, camo outfits and night vision goggles?" Ellen laughed as she disappeared down the hall heading for the shower, praising the man who took his volunteer job so seriously. "Want to join me, comrade?" It was that look from Ellen that convinced him, he needed a shower too.

Later, Ellen kissed Jack on the cheek and patted him on the bum as he made lunch for the two of them. Before lunch could be served, Jack left the room and returned a few minutes later with a book. He proceeded to eat while thumbing through the U.S. Chess Federation's Official Rules of the game. Later, he called Ed to give him an update on the new neighbors.

§

Jack walked the four blocks, to his new neighbor's home, with a bottle of red wine and the chess book of rules safely tucked away in his backpack. He noticed right away that the lawn had been mowed and weeds pulled from flower beds as he had requested. Jack had a smile of satisfaction as he made his way up the steps of Yuri and Ivan's home and made a mental note to mention the fine yard work to them. The front door swung open as he reached for the doorbell. "Come in, Jack. Welcome my new friend." Yuri stood back, stroking his mustache, as Jack entered for the second time. The aroma that hit him the moment he entered was not friendly. Jack tried not to react, but the stench came close to knocking him to the floor.

"I will take coat and pack, please." Yuri looked proud as he stood straight acting as the perfect greeter and host.

"Thank you. Oh, there's a bottle of red wine in the pack. I didn't know what to bring…"

"Is perfect for what Denis, I mean, Ivan, Denis is his middle name, is preparing for us, borshch!" Denis overheard the name slip that Boris made and smiled at how quickly he covered it up.

Jack had never heard of borshch, only that it smelled awful. The look on Jack's face caused Yuri to react. "Borshch is a favorite of mine, I hope you'll like it, my chess playing neighbor. Do you enjoy eating beets, Jack?" Jack had never judged his position on the matter of beets and told Yuri so, causing the man to nearly double over in laughter. "You are funny, Jack."

The men sat eating the soup that had taken Denis, aka Ivan, nearly all day to prepare. "I hope the smell from my cooking is not too offensive, Jack." Denis could tell that this could be the man's first experience with the Russian soup, which was a staple in his country. Jack surprised himself by asking for seconds as the offer was made, before clearing the table for after dinner drinks and setting up the chess board.

"So, Jack, you mentioned work in government, correct?" Yuri seemed very interested. Jack explained his position with the City Planning Department and his responsibilities. They talked for nearly an hour before Yuri excused himself under the pretext of having to pee, but in reality, had to reset his mustache, which began to slip because of all the heat in the room. Upon his return, Yuri announced that their game of chess should be played as an international contest!

"Ivan will be spectator, you and I will become international opponents, right Jack?" Yuri said this laughing as he brought out a bottle of Russian vodka. The wine Jack brought went basically untouched at dinner. Obviously, vodka was the Russian's drink of choice. *Should I have known?* Jack thought to himself as the chess pieces went into place on the board.

Jack had been a chess champion and president of Shadle Park High School's chess club. He'd dabbled in local competitions before meeting Ellen, but lost interest after college. "You are white, so begin our match comrade, err ah, Jack." Playing his first game in a long time felt good. To Jack, coming back to the game he'd spent more than a few years playing was like riding a bike, or so he thought. His counterpart across the table seemed to be heavily engrossed in Jack's moves. So much so, Yuri began to grunt and groan as Jack removed some of the black pieces from the board.

When Yuri's knights and one bishop were gone, and he only had his king and a few pieces left, he looked at Jack as though he would eat him for dessert, then quickly changed into a more peaceful mood. "You are good, my friend. I am in need of a better plan of attack. I surrender to you." The move surprised Jack. From where he sat, Yuri had at least two or three more moves before conceding the match.

"Let's drink to your health," Yuri suggested, setting up some small shot glasses." Jack normally drank beer, but he gave in to the man who seemed to enjoy the new rivalry. Things progressed rapidly after the first game. Two and a half hours later they were on their third match when Yuri's brother headed off to bed with one request of Jack; "Be careful, Yuri gets better the more he drinks." Denis may have appeared to be kidding, then he added:

"Nice to meet with you, Jack. Please to return back again soon so you can beat my brother at his own game." Yuri laughed and suggested they stop for a few minutes and talk.

The drinking continued with the conversation and Jack wondered if he could safely get up and move away from the table to the bathroom. When Jack returned, the two men sat at the kitchen island facing one another. The gas fireplace and one small kitchen lamp provided just enough illumination as Jack began to feel the booze taking over. "Tell me, Jack, what is it that you do for fun, play chess on the weekends?" Jack didn't want the man to know that he hadn't actually played for years. Instead, he told his Russian host about playing golf in the summer and then casually mentioned his recent comedy experience.

"You are comedian, Jack?" The man said it so loud, Jack thought he'd wake up Ivan or the neighbors. "No…not really. I just tried out with a group of other amateurs at a local club recently."

The big man slapped the kitchen island and laughed from deep down. "Now it all makes sense. You, Jack, are perfect person to be comedian. I knew there was something odd about you, my new friend. I mean that in a good way - believe me. Please don't take my words wrong, okay?"

Jack assured Yuri that no offense was taken, in fact, from his childhood, Jack had been told the same by his parents. When he shared that fact, Yuri laughed and asked Jack to share a few of his jokes.

Jack hesitated for a few seconds then began with: "Why did the chicken cross the road?" Yuri just looked and smiled, not answering. Jack nodded his head as if to encourage the man to respond. "Oh, I see, it is my turn. Yes, well, why *did* chicken cross road?"

Jack answered with a quick reply, "I don't know, I don't talk to chickens, that's why I'm asking you! If I talked to chickens and could actually understand and maintain a conversation with them, which I doubt would EVER happen, do you think I'd be here asking?" The man going by the name of Yuri began to laugh half way through Jack's response. Jack had the man on his heels so to speak. So, he kept going through what came next from his routine a few days ago on stage. Yuri finally held up a hand as if begging Jack to stop.

After things calmed down, Jack shared the fact that he wasn't completely confident in performing comedy. "What? Are you a crazy person, Jack? You are good. Very good." It became obvious to Jack that the vodka may have helped Yuri in his assessment of Jack's ability to be funny, but at that point he didn't really care. The bottle, which was full earlier, had, at best, two shots remaining. "I have to work in the morning, Yuri."

"Please, just a few more minutes (mee-nuts), Jack."

The older man looked tired all of a sudden. It could have been the chess matches he and Jack had played, each winning two and ending with a draw. That could have taken its toll, although Jack couldn't tell.

"Jack, you are good man." He stopped as his head dropped. "Yuri, are you okay? Should I get Ivan?" The Russian stood and backed away from the island, turning toward the back slider he asked: "Jack, can I trust you?" The two former strangers suddenly found a new focus as they looked at one another.

The comment surprised Jack. He didn't know what to say about whether the man could put his trust in Jack. He paused for a few more seconds and then spoke. "Yes, of course, Yuri." The big man looked up at the ceiling then turned to face Jack and removed his mustache. It was big and thick and looked as though it hurt as the adhesive gave way. "I am not - Yuri." As he spoke the words, Jack realized who the man looked like and before the Russian could utter another sound Jack spoke up. "No, no you're not. You're him, Boris Yeltsin." Jack heard his voice crack as he said the words, it was as if he stood watching the experience rather than participating in it. Jack felt numb as the wave of thought returned and he realized the significance of what he'd just said. He rose and stood next to the island, using it for support, as he faced the Russian leader. "Yes, I am he," Boris whispered as a complete look of relief overtook him. He smiled, reached across the island and shook Jack's hand. "Nice to be meeting you, Jack Templeman. The two men sat. Jack slower than Boris. "The man asleep in the next room is not my brother, he's my bodyguard and driver, Denis. We are to remain as Yuri and Ivan for the now, Jack. I hope this can be understood by you." Jack just nodded as Boris poured the last two shots.

"Denis and I are here in your Eagle Ridge, a place we like very much." Boris raised his glass and they clicked glasses as he continued. "We are under your federal government's protection." Jack did not see that coming and told Boris so. He couldn't take his eyes off the man the world had been chasing for the last week. "Okay, so we have the President of Russia living *right here in river city*." Boris just stared at Jack, not realizing he'd just referenced a line from the musical, *Music Man*. Both men were doing their darndest to stay focused after finishing off a quart of Stolichnaya.

So, is Denis armed?" "Yes, we both are, for protection." Jack's epiphany slowly overcame his normally carefree mood, replacing it with a heart-throbbing blood rush. The clock on the wall crept close to midnight as Jack sat in a house with two Russian fugitives, one of whom was an infamous foreign leader, targeted by a communist opposition intent on capturing or killing the man, on site, according to the nightly news. Yeltsin's demise depended on where he happened to be found.

"I hope you understand, Mr. President, that this is a bit much to take in all at once, especially after drinking that clear liquid of yours." Jack surprised himself by getting the words out. "I *do*, Jack. But I also trust you will tell no one until we are gone." The request carried a tremendous weight that Jack felt pour over him as he sunk down further into his seat. Jack sat there stunned taking a moment, trying to absorb the last few minutes. For once in his life – he had nothing to say. He downed a whole glass of water before commenting.

Jack assured Boris that his secret was safe and that he would be in touch the next day after work. He found the man compelling and surprisingly likable. Boris had unexpectedly reached out and lifted the monkey off of his own back and placed it unknowingly on Jack's. The more Jack thought about what Boris must be going through, the more he felt sorry for the man known around the world.

The walk home felt good. The evening air helped to revitalize Jack as he recounted the impact of what just happened. No one was to find out. Not even Ellen. Jack took a few more carefully constructed steps before stopping and turning. Looking at the newly mowed yard, now in compliance, he began to laugh to himself. *I just shared a bottle of vodka with the President of Russia.*

§

The next morning came too early. Jack literally dragged himself out of bed and off to work. He went through the motions of making revisions to the latest development plans, triple checking to make sure he didn't make any mistakes. He caught his second wind after lunch and as the day progressed, looked forward to another visit with Boris Yeltsin. The thought made him chuckle as Ed walked up to his desk. "What's so funny, Jack?" "Hey, Ed, sorry about skipping out on lunch today, I've been swamped. I ah, I was just thinking about appearing again at Peabody's." "You should Jack. There's another amateur night coming up Friday."

Jack waited a few minutes before calling Peabody's to make the arrangement to be in Friday night's line up. Jerry Peabody seemed more than pleased to hear from him. Jerry said he had good feedback from Jack's first appearance and intended to contact Jack to see if he had any interest. The conversation was very positive. It made Jack feel good, as good as he felt late last night with Boris's encouragement for Jack to "Keep going with what you believe in – and have passion for."

§

Ellen just sat and listened as Jack explained, very carefully, why he was going to spend more time with the men who had just moved into Eagle Ridge. Her antennae went up as she and Jack finished dinner. "What? Did you leave something over there last night?" "No, El, it's not that I left something, it's, well, it's more like I find the guy to be very interesting." Ellen slowly stopped and stared at Jack. She had transformed her face into *the look*. It didn't happen that often, but when it did the only thing Jack could do was stop talking and think. *Be careful, Jack, you promised.* They were in the middle of a stare down that made Jack sweat in places he didn't know he could. Until, Ellen finally relented. Her goofy husband's response made her smile. "Jesus, Jack, go, be with your new Russian friends. You are nuts – you know that, right?" Jack could breathe again, but he had to be careful, so he paced his response, "Yes… I… do." Then added, "Oh and by the way, I'm in the comedy line up for Friday at Peabody's."

"Great, Jack. I'll call around and see who wants to go with us. It'll be fun." The thought of inviting people to attend the show gave Jack an idea as he left.

§

The borshch smell still lingered as Denis welcomed Jack with a semi-frisking hug. He and Jack sat in the living room facing one another. "Can I bring you drink, neighbor?" Just water for now, thanks." Denis grinned as he turned away. Americans, obviously, were not used to starting their visits (veesits) with the other clear liquid. He left and came back with two waters. "I understand that Boris shared our true identities and what is happening here." Denis's statement caught Jack staring out the back window at a neighbor's fence that had a few boards missing. Grounds for his next HOA landscape cop visit. Staring straight ahead, Jack answered. "Ah, yes, in fact he did."

"I wish he had not, but he did. Now you look at my face – I am telling you something." Jack came out of his HOA observation stare, having felt a more serious tone in the Russian's voice. He adjusted his posture back to sitting stoic and attentive as the man with steel-gray eyes sent a riveting look his way. "This is serious situation we've found ourselves in, Jack. I like you, but you need to know, if anything goes bad and something happens to the man sleeping in the next room dies because of you, you will die too. Is that clear?" It didn't take Jack long to answer. "Yes, I-I understand. I assure you…" Before he could finish Boris walked into the room. Denis held up his hand to stop Jack from talking any further.

"Jack. Want to go round two with chess board?"

"Sure, Boris. You don't mind if I call you by your first name, sir?"

"Not at all." Boris used his arms freely as he pointed to each person, including himself. "We are in your territory, not ours. You are Jack, I am Boris, and he is Denis. I am, how you say, satisfied? that someone here knows who the hell we really are."

It was Boris's turn to give someone the evil eye. Evidently, Boris heard the last part of Denis and Jack's discussion. Denis looked away. He nodded his head at Jack and went to the kitchen to prepare their dinner. "We always eat later. And not to worry, no borscht tonight on menu. Come, let's go outside and sit on concrete slab." There were two chairs and a small table awaiting the two new friends. Boris poured two drinks, vodka of course, as the sun began to set in the west, off to their right. The shade of two Hawthorne trees and the drink made for a relaxing moment under a golden sky.

"Jack, you know why I'm here I assume." Jack nodded to Boris who continued. "But do you really know the truth? I will tell you." Boris, without hesitation, proceeded to share how much he envied Americans and their lifestyle. "You have everything. Free enterprise and democracy are good for you and they could, also, be good for Russia, in parts and pieces to begin." The President of Russia went on to explain why the USSR, along with its ideology, needed to evolve into something greater. He added that the younger generation wanted more out of life, which did not include living under the watchful eye of aging Communist leadership. "Communism is becoming, what you call, a *hard sell*. More and more people in my country, mostly younger, see how people in your country enjoy life: homeownership, an enormous quantity of food in large markets, fully-stocked stores, automobiles that most people can afford, technology… Freedom. Most important is Freedom. Do what they want and go where they want – when they want without asking permission. Communism will never promise all of that, but we can certainly become more lenient in certain ways."

Listening to Boris became difficult all of sudden. It was as if Jack didn't want to hear what Boris was saying. He could feel a spotlight hitting his face like at Peabody's. He began to truly feel the heat. The moment hit Jack like a blow to the head and he realized the importance of the discussion. Jack was listening on behalf of the whole world or at least those that were interested in liberty for all. He felt as if he had become the representative for all of the democratic nations of the world, and those that aspired to be.

The two neighbors talked for over an hour, until sunset faded and stars began to pop. The air temperature became less comfortable, quickly falling below fifty degrees. "Let's go in, Jack, and continue conversation, unless, I have spoken too much at you." Jack shook his head and assured Boris of his interest.

Jack had eaten, so he watched as the other two shared a meal of potato soup. "You two are going to go hungry if you keep eating soup," Jack joked. Boris responded right away, and taking Jack seriously, countered with: "Oh, no, Jack, we had American cheese burgers for lunch. Some lady named Wendy made them for us."

Denis cleaned up as Jack and Boris set up the chess

board. This time the game was not so intense, which made the international aspect of the competition more enjoyable. After the first few moves, the two men relaxed, enjoying each other's company even more. To the surprise of each man, and Denis who sat close by reading, they shared personal information. Denis stopped reading at one point and just looked at the man who had been known as a stand-up guy when he wasn't falling down drunk. Boris said, "You know, Jack, I have reputation for drinking more than I should. I enjoy vodka same as this chess game we are playing. I wonder, is it wrong to find equal pleasure in those things?" Jack looked at the man, not really knowing what to say, so he smiled and held the man's gaze for an instant before responding. "Your move, sir."

Jack felt comfortable telling Boris about the pregnancy that he and Ellen lost last year. "I am sad for you and your wife, Jack, but there is hope – always hope. My life meant less until we had children. Then life becomes bigger when my children began having children. That is when you know why we were created, Jack. Our children make us happy, and grandchildren add joy and wonder to life." Jack smiled and sat up more. Discussing the merits of Parenthood with the President of Russia, overtook his next move, so Jack sat back. "We plan to try again soon." Jack looked away for a few seconds before going on. "I appreciate you sharing your feelings, sir." "Oh, please, call me, Boris, Jack."

All three men laughed heartily as they sat visiting in the living room next to the fire. Both Boris and Denis were strangers to this place that served as a location of refuge for the leader of a country with eleven time zones, and his protector. They seemed to visibly relax as the conversation continued until Jack raised a question that he'd wanted to ask for some time. Denis excused himself, picking plates and cups up as he left.

"Boris, do you know any jokes?" There was a pause as Boris looked around the room then over at the kitchen where Denis began to wash dishes. "Yes. Yes. But you need to know, something first, Jack. Boris took a big drag off his cigarette, exhaled, and in one motion, moved closer to Jack's chair. Looking straight into Jack's eyes whispered, "There isn't much to laugh about in Russia these days." The silence in the room enhanced the man's comment. After another drag on his cigarette, Boris continued, "We need more reasons to laugh, more importantly we need to also understand why." Boris adjusted his sitting position, looking up at the ceiling with a smile coming on. "Jack, do you know why chicken is crossing road?" Jack smiled. He hoped the man he now sat facing would come up with something funny. "No, why, Boris, why did the chicken cross the road?" "Because he is scared of me – HE IS CHICKEN!" Jack had to admit he'd never heard THAT particular version before and laughed at Boris's unique delivery of an old standard.

Boris's look changed to serious and Jack readied himself for, exactly what, he didn't know. "Jack, The USSR is more a patchwork quilt comprising a huge landmass, Russia, with neighboring satellite countries. Each has experienced war, impoverished citizens, and decaying infrastructure. That is why I've been elected, to do something about these problems and to lead my country into the next century. People who are after me want to go back to old ways by putting the quilt back together. That's why it's difficult for me to find a joke for you tonight, but I promise you, one day we will be a country that enjoys more in life, especially jokes. The room went silent once again as the fire's fan became the only sound.

Jack apologized to Boris about having to leave earlier than the first night they played chess. "Because of you I'm in the lineup for Friday's Amateur Night at Peabody's, the comedy club I mentioned last night." "Good, I shall be there to laugh at your jokes." "What? Wait, Boris. Can you go out like that?" Boris leaned over to within inches of Jack's face and slowly replied, "I have Denis and that horrible mustache, both will keep me safe." Denis looked up from the kitchen, took off his apron and added: "We've been locked up here for too many days, Jack. We need to get out. Where is this Peabody place?"

# Chapter 7

## PEABODY'S LAUGH EMPORIUM - AMATEUR NIGHT

Jerry Peabody rubbed his hands together in satisfaction as he finished putting the Friday night's "Laugh Card" together. He placed the lineup sheet in the old wicker note basket on his desk. The basket had been given to him by his grandfather as a joke, according to Jerry's mother. The memory of his "papa" made him smile, as did the inscription stamped on the bottom of the basket: Best Efforts Only.

Jerry retired early from the Spokane Police Department at the age of 48, two years earlier. As a lead homicide detective he'd helped solve enough crime, it was time to shine a brighter light on life, and his wife agreed. For years, Jerry wanted to own and manage a bar like his father and grandfather did, and with one difference – the addition of a stage for comedy. Jerry contacted an old friend, Ed La Drew, who worked in the Planning Department at City Hall. He asked Ed if he knew of any sites available in the downtown area. It took Ed less than a week to find the perfect location, not far from City Hall on Spokane Falls Blvd. When Jerry saw the old brick building for the first time, he knew it had possibilities, but it needed work. The dropdown ceilings had to be removed and certain walls had to be eliminated in order to make room for the stage, kitchen and bar. It took six months and most of their savings, but the Peabody's opened the most unique comedy club in the Inland Northwest. Jerry couldn't believe all that work happened nearly three years ago.

Jerry's grandfather never saw the place, but his father comes every Wednesday and most Friday nights for amateur night and to see touring big name talent. It always pleased Jerry when the lineup looked good as it did for tonight. The place will fill up fast and the laughs will be bouncing off the walls. Happy crowds ate and drank more, that was a given. But what Jerry liked more than anything was word of mouth advertising. People telling their family and friends about the good time they had at Peabody's.

The entertainment card listed the names and times of the amateur comics for the night's show. Wednesday was normally Amateur Night, but Jerry changed the rotation to Friday, primarily because a big name from California canceled late. Although Friday had become synonymous with featuring a national talent, Jerry took a chance. Besides, he had great audience feedback from the previous Amateur Night, two weeks earlier. And from where Jerry stood, behind the stage curtain, he'd made the right move. The place was filling up with new faces. That was the purpose of the event, to bring in new people.

Comedy lounges around the country depended on nights

like this to "pick up the week" from slower nights. Weekends were normally sellouts, especially if they had a nationally recognized comedian headlining the show.

One of the new performers, Jack Templeman, was someone Jerry especially looked forward to seeing again. He placed Templeman in the middle of the pack, a good place for beginners, also doing his friend, Ed La Drew, a favor.

§

"Hurry up, Jack, we're going to be late," Ellen shouted from the kitchen. Jack was in the bedroom staring at the mirror going through his note cards of jokes. "Be right there, El." He placed the cards in a manilla folder, car keys on top of the folder. Not that he would forget his cards, that would never happen, which made him laugh out loud. Jack was in a good mood, ready for the night and hoping not to throw up.

They parked the car in Jack's reserved spot behind City Hall and walked the four blocks to Peabody's. The old location turned comedy club pub had been a popular jewelry store back in the forties and fifties. Since Jerry Peabody and his wife poured a big chunk of their life savings into the remodel, formerly known for glitz and glamour, was becoming a downtown fixture - again. Ed told Jack that the business was finally turning a profit for his long-time friend. Ed and Jerry had known each other since high school at Lewis and Clark. Ed always knew that Jerry would be successful. Jerry played football and encouraged Ed to turn out for sports. Ed liked football, but not as a player. He enjoyed the various plays on offense and defense and drew his favorites for Jerry in their mechanical drawing class, which got Ed into trouble when

Ed turned in homework with x's and o's on it. Ed eventually joined the school's newest sport program, archery, which matched his need to draw straight lines and achieve his goal to hit any target that life put in front of him.

The minute Ellen and Jack walked into Peabody's Jack's nerves hit him full on. Ellen recognized the moment Jack began to lose his cool – his face froze like the Joker's, almost unrecognizable. "Jack, Jack, honey, are you okay?" It took a few beats for Jack's facial muscles to relax as they walked to a table where Ed and Janice waited. "There he is, the man of the hour!" Ed proclaimed as he, too, noticed the odd expression on Jack's face. "Jack, you alright?" Ellen had to intervene with a wave of her hand, "Oh, he's fine, Ed, just having a mild stroke, he'll be ready to go by showtime."

Two men who recognized Jack the minute he walked in were sitting in the back row. Both wore hats, one had a mustache, the other had on dark glasses. It was an old school KGB trick. Wearing dark glasses allowed Denis to watch the entire place without scrutiny or suspicion. Both nursed pints of beer and kept their distance from the others as best they could. Denis, wearing a Mariner baseball cap, knew their government caretakers were close by - he had that sense about him. He'd kept a steady eye on the rearview mirror as he led them on what they thought would be a routine drive to the store or along High Drive. Then, at the last minute, Denis made a change and a few quick turns ending up parked in a lot two blocks away from Peabody's. He and Boris made their way to Peabody's just in time to find a couple of back row seats. Boris hoped the U.S. Government people would keep their cool and have a few good laughs during the evening. Boris's bodyguard pointed to two men, dressed in suits, across the room, standing close to the bar. "We have company, sir."

Boris acknowledged Denis by tipping his fedora, provided by the U.S. Government, and a click of a glass.

Jack eventually loosened up, which required one beer and some deep breathing techniques that Janice suggested. The master of ceremonies, a fellow cop and friend of Jerry's from New York, opened the show right on time, 8pm. By then Jack had a beer and felt much better about being in the room and performing. "I'm fine guys. I've got my cards and my lucky charm." Jack pulled out a distress whistle he used when he went snow skiing. "You're not serious, Jack," Ellen playfully suggested with a laugh. When Jack started to put the whistle in his mouth, she grabbed it from him and threw it in her purse.

The master of ceremonies completed his opening act, which resulted in cheers and applause. "And now for the real talent this evening - our amateurs! This week only – Welcome to Friday Amateur Night!" More applause. "And we have some very funny people, four ladies and six gentlemen ready to entertain you with their wit and charm. Without further ado, give a big Peabody's welcome to Miss Yolanda Jefferson." Jack's eyes watched every move the lady made coming on to the stage. She was big, black and very sassy. Yolanda walked up to the mic, looked out over the crowd and with a heavy, sexy whisper, greeted the audience with: "Well, hello there." A few seconds went by, and after a scattering of polite laughter she changed voices with a quick click to a lighter octave followed by, "I haven't seen this many white people since the power company came to shut off my electricity." (Huge laughs) "I mean I know it takes three or four of y'all to change a light bulb, but that many (she points around the room) to flip a damn switch?"

Needless to say, Yolanda was a big hit. It seemed like

she went longer than the time limit they were given, twenty minutes. But Jerry wasn't about to intervene when the rafters were shaking. Jack took a few deep breaths to remain calm, knowing he had to step up his game. He couldn't just tell a joke, he had to do more, but what? There were three more performers before he'd be called to the stage.

Each person following Yolanda did a fair job. One poor fellow, Gary somebody, was so nervous he mostly shook out of control, which, oddly, became part of his act. He looked and sounded like Don Knotts, a.k.a. Deputy Barney Fife, trying to explain himself to Sheriff Andy Taylor. His jokes weren't that funny, but his delivery was hilarious. Jack made a decision then and there, after watching Yolanda and Gary, to make an addition to his act, *performance.*

"And now, a man who comes highly recommended, right out of City Hall. Let's give a big Peabody's welcome for Mr. Jack Templeman." Jack pushed his chair out, catching part of the carpet, causing the chair to fall down behind him. When he went to retrieve it, his cards fell out of the breast pocket in his sport coat and onto the floor. He didn't have time to pick them up and decided he'd wing it before the applause died. Besides, only one contestant had used cards up to that point and it didn't go over well at all. *Let's do this.*

Jack stood, straightened his chair, and made his way up to the stage after pushing his chair forward and giving his table a thumbs up. His heart was beating faster than ever, which would have been okay if it weren't in his throat. Jack made it up the small ramp to the stage no problem. He had the first lines to his bit ready to go. He also had one thought that kept pounding in his head, performance, performance, performance!

"Good evening. *God why is my voice so high?* Jack

immediately lowered his voice and continued. "Like Jerry said, I'm a City Planner. Yes, I'm the guy responsible for naming your communities and your streets." (Some boos, some mumbling comments, a few laughs) In the style of Bob Newhart, Jack, shielded his eyes with one hand and asked if anyone in the audience had some suggestions for good street names. A man sitting close to Boris and Denis's table began to mumble something to the others sitting with him. They all laughed. One of them reached over, a woman, trying to hold him back. Instead, the man smiled, finished his beer. Boris watched as the man wiped his lips and stood.

"You bet, how about Mother F***er Drive," the big guy yelled from the back. The crowd responded with hoots and whistles. Denis just stared at the man, his hand checking for the gun at the small of his back.

Jack waited a few seconds to let the crowd noise die out, then replied: "Nope, sorry, MF Drive is already taken, that's the street my boss lives on." That line resulted in the biggest laugh of the night, causing Ed to nearly topple over backward in his chair laughing. Jack hesitated. Boris, sitting on the edge of his seat, quietly urged him to speak, "Do something, say anything. "You are funny, Jack," he quietly whispered, leaning forward. After overhearing Boris's whisper, a lady, who'd been admiring the two husky gents sitting close by in the crowded environment, asked Boris, "Forgive me, I couldn't help but hear you. Are you related to Mr. Templeman?" It was an opening line that Denis read as she continued to flex her facial muscles. Denis put his hand on Boris's chest and answered for him in heavy Russian. "We are neighbors." The lady immediately snapped back into her chair, as if told to go away, looked at her girlfriend and quickly downed the rest of her Chablis.

Jack smoothly adjusted the mic on the stand and went with the audience instead of his notes. *Performance*. The funny street names he'd planned to offer, became more vulgar instead. He nodded his head and proceeded: "But Shits Creek Way is still available…" Jack went through a whole series of slang words synonymous with the spirit of the first suggestion made by the big mouth in the back, which brought the house down, including the two Russian fugitives who were patting each other on the back and high fiving the people around them.

As a result, Jack's first ten minutes stretched to twenty and went by faster than he'd anticipated. Jerry came up on stage and put his arm around Jack, suggesting that if he did any more stand up, people would be passing out. When he looked out at the audience, Jack could barely see Ellen, Ed and Janice standing and cheering along with the rest.

About an hour later, when all the comedians had completed their routines, Jerry Peabody led the audience in voting for the best act. The crowd started shouting out various names of the contestants and Ellen thought Jack's name could be heard above the rest. Jerry quieted the audience with a few jokes of his own while his crew set up the meter off to the side of the stage. The meter consisted of a vertical line in the middle of a board with a white background. The line had three sections labeled; low, medium and high. A stream of bright orange light would rise up the meter in reaction to the audience's applause.

The applause meter was pressed into action and when it was all over Jack came in second to Yolanda. Jack had to agree. "The lady had a natural style that made you laugh before she even opened her mouth." Driving home he and Ellen couldn't stop reliving the evening. "You were quick on your feet, Jack. Your timing was perfect, once you let the butterflies out."

He had to admit that the evening went better than he'd expected. Jack surprised himself by feeding off the responses of the audience and being extemporaneous. At one point, through all of the laughable chaos, Jack thought he heard the familiar deep-set laugh of his new neighbor.

§

The Canadian border lies approximately one hundred and thirty miles directly north of Spokane, Washington. The State of Washington and the Canadian Province of British Columbia share the border with 13 crossings over 427 miles of mostly rugged mountainous terrain. One of those border crossings, Metaline Falls, WA across from Nelway, B.C., sits directly north of Spokane and is one of the least traveled of the 13. The corridor on the U.S. side is shared by two highways, 31 and 2. The combination of these, mostly, two lane stretches, is practically a straight shot into the heart of Spokane, often referred to by the American locals as the Canadian Throughway. There are plenty of reasons for both sides to cross the border back and forth. Skiing, golfing, camping, commerce, and generally just getting away, make for good times and friendly relations between the two countries. Americans often find the exchange of funds to their advantage over their Canadian counterparts, who also just need a change of pace.

The day after Jack Templeman's successful comedy night, a man and a woman crossed the border as Canadian citizens coming to the States on holiday. The U.S. Border guard had no issue with their credentials or the lovely smile on the lady's face as the guard gate rose and he wished them well. The guard even waved as they drove off on their journey south in their charcoal gray midsize truck, with a small bed camper.

If the border guard had spent any time searching through their camper, he may have found sophisticated field equipment and weapons used often by the two highly-trained assassins. The ordinance had been cleverly hidden, of course, and would have taken more time at the small border crossing known for quick glances and friendly waves. The two fake vacationers returned the smile, knowing they were safely across and that the mission they were assigned would receive international attention when completed. "Flirtatious border guards are my favorite," the woman offered as she rubbed moisturizing lotion on her hands and arms. Albert found it hard to get used to Irina's distracting deep sexy voice as he clicked on the high beams for better vision. The sky would be lightening up soon and driving in this unfamiliar territory would improve, at least he hoped so. Albert prided himself on being able to focus on what he was assigned to do, which included being able to see the old highway they were now heading south over as directed. What he didn't count on was attempting to keep focus while working with a beautiful, albeit, dangerous woman.

Albert busied himself by driving as Irina traded the hand lotion for an international satellite phone. It became her responsibility to check in with their contact in Moscow at regular intervals.

Their mark had been located, along with his bodyguard, in Eastern Washington, more specifically in the city of Spokane. The two Russian agents had flown into Vancouver, British Columbia a few days apart, each from different parts of the world. Albert went further into Canada and spent a few days in northern B.C. before meeting Irina in Nelson as directed.

Irina Dustakova, originally from Bulgaria, spent the last six weeks in London on a romantic assignment with a member of the British Parliament. He had been on the Russian payroll, but his time, unfortunately for him, had run its course. The poor bloke knew more than the Communist Party leaders were comfortable allowing, so he had to go before he could become a double agent. Irina watched from the bed they were sharing, as the man's eyes grew lifeless with each twist of her pearl-handle knife. Once that mission was complete, she had to move on before the ranking member of the British Conservative Party was found completely drained, the victim of a deadly assault. Irina added, yet, another perfect result to her long list of accomplishments before turning 30. She had another year to go. The thought created a smile as she boarded her first-class flight to Vancouver.

*Perfect timing,* Albert Trejenko thought as he received the notice for his next assignment. He met Irina in Nelson, B.C. the day she arrived. He'd been spending time further north in British Columbia after an assignment in the Philippines, training radicals on the techniques of sniper warfare. His style was more military and involved long-range sniper fire as opposed to Irina's closer encounters. The two were a deadly combination with a 100% kill rate. Their superiors were more than confident that Albert and Irina would succeed in this extraordinary mission. After a few failed attempts on Russian soil, Communist Party leaders considered the Spokane assignment to be a welcomed opportunity and expected a successful conclusion.

Their target location shouldn't be difficult to find and in the next few hours, before arriving in Spokane, their Moscow contact would report back with more exact coordinates.

Albert and Irina looked the part of husband and wife. The truth was – they were actually competitors in their jobs as assassins. Each knew of the other, in fact, each had trained under one of the most scrupulous killers in the KGB system, Admiral Deuskov. The Admiral had many credits to his thirty-year resume, but the one he was most proud of was consulting the Red Sparrow School. Young women, like Irina, were carefully trained to use their minds and bodies to spy and kill. The Admiral didn't invent the process, he just made it more sophisticated, which Irina thought of as she and her handsome driver drove on over American soil. She wouldn't be spying for information with this engagement, no, Irina would be aiming to kill a man who dedicated himself to removing the heart and soul of Russia. The evil smile that appeared on her perfectly shaped lips did not go unnoticed by Albert. Driving in the dark can be monotonous, so he decided to find out more about his lovely companion as the sky began to lighten up.

"You have been away on assignment lately, Irina." "Yes, my dear Albert. And you know I can't discuss any of the particulars." Of course, Albert knew. Deep down he might have been trying to test her, but in reality, his query was an honest attempt to make conversation. Assassins were a testy bunch. Albert had to be careful trying to get to know the woman he'd heard so much about. What they did for a living, for Russia and the expansion of Communism around the world, was best kept secret. However, the drive would be longer, more mysterious, and extremely boring if they couldn't talk or exchange ideas. Albert gave her a look of frustration. "Oh, Albert, I don't mean to annoy you, let's do talk about what you've been up to dear one."

"Touché, Irina my love." She chuckled at Albert's fake loving remark and touched his leg, which caused the truck to increase in speed momentarily. They talked about their current assignment instead. This job had the expectation of a *quick in and out easy kill* written all over it. "There is not that much intel on this one, Irina. We are to locate the target and make the hit within twenty-four hours of finding him." "I'm so glad you are up to speed, Albert. Have you ever been assigned duty in the United States?" Albert shook his head and asked if she had ever touched American soil, as she slowly lifted her hand away from his leg. "First for me too."

Albert made a comment about them experiencing an assignment together for the first time, which had some sexual overtones wrapping its naughty wings around the expression. Irina told her slightly older companion to keep his eyes on the road and drive, "Like a good boy should." They both agreed they'd like to spend more time in the States, but understood the need to disappear quickly the way they came.

Albert liked to drive, especially at night. Night time provided a cloak that he enjoyed wearing whenever he worked. Darkness also matched his personality and gave him time to think. However, watching the yellow line that divided the small, two-lane, highway that particular evening caused Albert to question his current assignment, which he never did before. A recuring line now kept coming at him like the yellow one with evenly spaced segments on the highway – why us - why us – why us?

In the last two years, before his assignment in the Philippines, Albert spent more time in Europe, causing trouble and confusion for countries allied against Yeltsin.

Most of his assignments involved English, French and German counter intelligence operations. Not only was this his first kill and escape assignment involving a partner, the kill involved a Russian leader. He looked over and caught Irina humming with soft jazz playing in her headphones. He tapped her on the shoulder, she responded by turning her head slowly, removing one earpiece, and staring at him with her head lowered in anticipation.

"There must be a reason *we've* been selected to eliminate Russia's President, Irina." "Stop it. You are reading my mind, Comrade," she responded softly.

§

Jack and Dash were walking one of their regular routes in Eagle Ridge, heading for Whispering Park. The recreational area sported an outdoor arena with rolling grass mounds as seating for two hundred, a covered patio for community picnics, a disc golf course, and several, strategically located poop bag dispensers for dog walkers. Jack enjoyed walking through the area, especially early in the morning before work. That's why he suggested that Boris meet with him there, at a particular picnic table overlooking a broad expanse of park grass. The partially wooded park accommodated participants in, soccer, field hockey, flag football, volleyball and Dash's favorite obstacle course, that involved chasing, soccer balls, footballs, volleyballs, squirrels, and the occasional marmot.

Jack and Dash slowly made their way up the meandering graveled slope to one of their favorite picnic tables. Dash checked out the nearby waste can while Jack settled on the bench side with a sweeping view, checking phone messages.

Off in the distance, Boris and Denis made their way down a gravel path surrounded by large pine trees that swayed gently as the morning sun's warmth began to spread with the breeze.

"Good morning my comedic friend," came Boris's deep-throated greeting. "Yuri, Ivan, good morning." Boris smiled and nodded as if thanking Jack for using their pseudo names. Dash noticed the men and raced to greet them as well. "Dash, you are energetic this morning," Boris said as he rubbed his furry admirer behind the ears. Dash's left back leg pounded the ground in response. Denis walked around the area checking out the perimeter before taking a seat across from Jack. "You were very good last night on stage, Jack." Denis, slow and deliberate in movements, extended that same control in his conversation. Jack noticed that he held back, as you would expect, in the presence of his noble charge and President. Jack still had trouble calling the man by his first name.

"Jack, you were the best of all your competitors last night. Denis and I believe you should have won all competition, how do you say? With your hands over? "Oh, you mean, hands down?" "Yes. Hands down!" Boris let go of Dash and sat next to Denis facing Jack.

"Have you heard any more about your status in Russia, Boris? I hope you don't mind if I ask." "No. I mean, yes, of course it is appropriate for you to wonder about us." Boris looked at the powder blue sky, then over at Denis as he offered what he knew. "Denis and I have been through many tough moments together, haven't we, my friend?" Boris touched Denis's folded hands on the table as he looked back to Jack. "We heard this morning, from our contacts, to be on alert. Evidently, people close to us have been tortured recently, poor souls. As a result, they may have provided the wrong people with my location."

Jack could only stare at the two men facing him. He didn't know what to say, resulting in a few moments of quiet. Silence was broken suddenly by Dash's alert barking, which made all three men jump and Denis to go for his gun. The lady walking her dog didn't notice the gun, only three guys sitting on a picnic bench talking. One of the men held a little Westie on a leash. Is that Ellen Templeman's husband? Who are the other two? Dash's bark faded when it became evident the people walking by posed no problem. "'Morning, Jack, have a nice day." Jack smiled and waved as she passed by.

"So, you, we, should all be on alert," Jack uttered with a blank expression. The look on his face registered Jack's disbelief, losing most of its color. His picnic table companions knew, full-well, what it was like to be hunted, chased, and living at the behest of others as escapees.

Boris cleared his throat and with a fatherly-like expression, did his best to reassure Jack. "Because of recent developments in Russia, Denis and I plan to leave as soon as two days from now. Plans are underway, Jack. There have been people watching over us while we've been here. Those overseers, mostly from your government, are now on high alert." High alert? That sounded like serious trouble from where Jack sat.

In the distance, across the large expanse of grass, sat a dark colored Suburban. The people inside monitored the three men in the park. The one with a spotting scope made a remark about the cute dog. "Sargent, the dog is the least of our concerns. Focus. The latest communication from the Pentagon warned of operatives possibly headed our way." Receiving information classified as an Urgent Alert, was a major concern. The officers and staff charged with keeping "eyes on" the target knew all about major concerns. More importantly, they also knew that the man dressed in a blue and white exercise outfit with the fake mustache, sitting at the picnic table with two others and a dog, must fly back home, alive, or there would be repercussions. This operation was the most important of Bernard Jackson's career. The agent sitting close to Jackson commented, "I guess Boris Yeltsin's life is important enough, sir." "Keep your opinion to yourself, Sargent. That's not for you to decide," came Jackson's quick reply. *It will all be over soon.*

More people appeared in the park as the threesome's visit came to an end. The men had been sitting for about half an hour. Denis stood, stretching his legs as Jack and Boris scheduled one last chess match for that evening. "The game calms my nerves, especially if I win (ween), Jack," Boris offered. "But only if you feel safe, my funny friend."

Jack's concern for his new Russian chess mate now registered emotionally. He wanted to say something profound, presidents and dignitaries deserved that, at least some did. He walked with the two gentlemen to the edge of an overlook above a small amphitheater. Jack felt a sudden rush of concern, not just for him personally, but for everyone that lived in Eagle Ridge. The sense of responsibility he had volunteering on the Landscaping Committee just ramped up a hundred times. Knowing the man who lived down the street made him more nervous than he ever could remember. It felt to Jack as if he was the only person who knew that a nuclear device was about to be detonated in Whispering Pines Park and he was helpless to tell anyone. As his two neighbors started walking, Jack bent down and looked at Dash who gave him an expectant look. "Okay, little man, what should I do?"

Television news reports regarding Yeltsin were less frequent and the rebellious situation appeared to be calming, at least in the media. Those thoughts, plus how he was going to play chess against the man one more time, ran through his head. Jack and Dash said their good-byes and made their way home. As Jack and Dash started down the familiar sloping gravel trail, everything looked new around him. He saw a stand of trees and the small exercise court, as if for the first time. And suddenly Jack knew he had something more to say. The two Russians were still within sight when Jack turned and shouted. "See you tonight, Yuri."

§

Wednesday came just in time – Ellen's night to go with girlfriends to workout at the gym. It pleased her that Jack would have something to do with his new friends while she caught up with the latest conversation going around by spinning. It did seem a little unusual that he'd been spending so much time lately with the two men who were new to the neighborhood. Normally, Jack would make contact with new residents and check in on an as needed basis. She also wondered where they were from and if they had family in the area? The HOA had asked Jack to introduce new residents during various outdoor events like Friday Night Movies, fun runs, and community barbecues. The purpose was to make the newbies meet their neighbors and feel a part of the Eagle Ridge community. It also gave Jack an opportunity to be in front of an audience. Ellen made a mental note to ask Jack about his new friends, later, after her gym class.

Jack fed Dash and let him out into the backyard to do his

thing before leaving to play chess with Boris. As he changed his outfit into something more casual, he felt as if he was forgetting something. The thought quickly vanished when he heard Dash barking outside. As he headed from the bedroom the doorbell rang. Checking the peephole, he could see it was Ed with a six pack in hand. Jack opened the door at the same time he remembered what he'd completely forgotten. "Ed! I'm a turd." "At least you finally admit it, Jack, about damn time, man." Jack froze, Ed laughed and waited and then noticed the extremely blank look on Jack's face. "Oh, you forgot."

"Yes, look, I'm sorry."

"So, we won't be watching the boxing match tonight after all? Jack, tonight is the big Russian against the American, remember?"

"That's ironic."

"What?" Jack explained that he'd made a prior commitment to the new guys down the block.

Ed's look made Jack feel worse than bad. "Hey, how about...can we reschedule?" "The fight? Ah, no, don't believe we can make that happen, Jack."

Instead, Ed suggested Jack take him along and introduce him to the new neighbors. Jack's look told Ed that something was going on, something that might require some explanation. The two men stood in the doorway, Ed looking at Jack, and Jack looking at his feet.

"Jack?"

"Ah, yeah, I'm thinking." Ed could tell that Jack had a hard time saying no, which wasn't at all like him. Finally, Jack looked up and whispered, "Can you keep a secret?"

Ed worked his way across the threshold, put the beer down, held his hands straight out from his sides and turned his head slightly in an, are you kidding me? gesture.

Jack felt a tremendous relief when he shared who the new residents were and that no one knew about it but them. "Boris, 'I want to be more like a capitalist' Yeltsin? Boris, 'Everyone in the world is looking for me' Yeltsin? The escaped leader of Russia?" "Yes, Ed, that Boris Yeltsin. And his bodyguard Denis."

Jack knew that in a short time, Boris Yeltsin would be on his way, so what did it matter if Ed was aware of his location? The fact was, Ed would be staying, Boris would be the one leaving. They packed up the beer and headed out.

Jack felt a little tense walking up to Boris's front door with Ed. He hoped that he wouldn't cause the two Russians any more concern than they already had. When Denis came to the door his smile faded as he opened it slowly. "Hey, Ivan. This, this is one of my neighbors, yours too. Denis's expression didn't change as Jack turned and pulled Ed forward in the same way a magician pulls a rabbit out of his hat. Ed, Ed La Drew." Denis looked at Ed, Ed looked up at Denis. "We bring beer!" Ed held up the six pack as Denis allowed the two to pass with one hand and the other at his lower back over a loaded pistol.

Boris waited in the living room, without his mustache, as the three men entered. He spoke slow and deliberate as if looking for an answer. "Jack, I see you brought a friend." Jack nervously made the introductions. A sudden realization came over Boris. He signaled to Denis that there was no reason for concern and his stern look changed to a smile. "Wait a minute. I see you at the Peabody's place, right?" "Yes, sir, your Presidency," Ed's words stumbled out of his mouth, which was unusual for the normally clear - thinking Ed. Both Jack and Ed kept an eye on Denis, who continued to wear the expression of a musclebound bodyguard, right out of a James Bond movie.

Boris broke the tension. "Come, come in and sit (seet) down, gentlemen. I'm guessing Jack told you who we really are." Jack nodded and Boris understood. "We won't be neighbors for much longer, Mr. La Drew?" Ed nodded. He couldn't take his eyes off Boris after shaking hands, as they made their way to their seats. After a minute, he managed to utter; "It's really you." Boris looked around the room, to the side and back behind himself. Then answered, "Yes, Mr. La Drew, it is me. You were expecting your own President maybe?" Jack and Ed looked at one another and laughed along with Boris – even Denis cracked a smile.

It took Ed a few more minutes to lower his bright wide-eyed gaze, close his mouth, and take a sip of beer. He watched as the chess board came into view. Jack and Boris sat at the dining room table across from each other with a pendant light chandelier hanging over the middle of the table. The room took on a certain mood with the chandelier the only source of light. It felt to Ed as though he was about to witness an international competition involving Bobby Fischer and Boris Spassky, former American and Russian chess grandmasters. Ed and Denis relaxed, one on each open side of the dining table, as spectators, while Jack and Boris settled into their chairs. The table looked even more official with the addition of Jack's timer, used to keep the match moving. All conversation stopped before Jack made the first move and hit the timer.

The black Suburban stationed outside for Boris's protection, drove slowly past. "They're playing chess again, sir," the officer with the headphones reported. Bernard Jackson responded with, "I'm surprised that Boris allowed

Jack to bring a friend. I mean, we know he's no threat, but why didn't Denis at least pat him down?" "Pretty poor security if you ask me, sir." They only had another thirty-six hours of surveillance scheduled, so it didn't really matter to Jackson if one of the neighbor's came by for a visit. Not revealing the identity of the man behind the fake mustache is what mattered. It had also surprised Jackson, but he couldn't stop the two men from entering the house. It would have given their position away. They would just keep watch and make sure no other neighbors came calling. "This will be over soon," came out of Jackson's mouth before he could stop it. The man on the headphones turned and looked at Jackson. "Pardon, sir?" "Never mind, Sargent," Jackson said with a smile.

Chapter 8

EAGLE RIDGE

Eagle Ridge suddenly turned into a tourist destination for Russians. Unfortunately, none of the visitors were intending to lay down roots or really stay that long. The latest pair to join the foreign travelers had a more sinister reason to drop by. Albert and Irina had twenty-four hours to, literally, kill some time. It was their assignment, which they aimed to complete without delay. The quiet community located on the south side of Spokane would, hopefully, never know. The people living there could go on with their lives without the threat of harm, unless they happened to be in the way. There were contingencies made for collateral damage, which sometimes, unfortunately, happened. Direct orders from Moscow made it clear that this assignment must be a clean hit and run. A messy international scene would be frowned upon by the Communist Party. The Kremlin already found itself in an embarrassing situation, having Boris Yeltsin successfully disappear. They didn't need any more negative or embarrassing publicity.

§

Albert drove the truck slowly in the early morning sun. Irina called out a set of directions to Albert that she had written down a few minutes earlier after a satellite phone call from their contact. The truck wound its way up Eagle Ridge Drive. Albert kept leaning forward looking up as well as out to the left, Irina looking to the right for street names.

"Albert, what are you doing, looking up so much?" "I am watching for eagles as well as addresses. I have never seen the bird, but would like to witness such a sight." "We haven't time to bird watch, Comrade, just drive."

§

Jack's concern about Eagle Ridge becoming an international target, grew as he reviewed his conversation with Boris and Denis from the night before. So much so that he convinced Ed to take a sick day and help him think. Jack had a plan of his own; keep Boris safe until his departure. It was the only thing he could think of doing for his community and his new friend and confidant. The chance meeting with his Russian neighbor made a major impact on Jack's life. The more he thought about it the more he considered what was said during their times together. Jack smiled to himself, thankful for knowing the man.

Boris and Jack played the previous night until midnight. Each won two matches and called their time together an *international draw*. Ed and Denis drank beer and cheered the two competitors on, as the house continued to be monitored by the small government force outside.

During the evening, Boris's conversation drifted into the political situation that he now faced in his homeland. Denis remained silent watching Ed's every move, even though Boris felt comfortable around Jack's friend. The encouragement came mostly from Jack with supporting questions coming from Ed. As far as Ed was concerned, the evening was surreal. He minored in Russian history and studied overseas. When Boris made it sound as if his enemies were everywhere, Ed's ears really perked up. "So, Mr. President, you feel uncomfortable everywhere you go?" "Yes, Ed (Id). I can tell you times I have traveled and there were signs, phone calls, notes, that came my way urging *Yeltsin to die a dreadful death*. "You don't think the same could possibly happen here? In Eagle Ridge I mean." Ed had such a look of concern, Boris just smiled and suggested that he felt better about being in this place every day. And then he added with raised arms and shrugged shoulders, "But you never know in this crazy world of ours."

The comment didn't help comfort Ed, but he tried not to show it, especially after trading glances with Denis during the evening. Instead, he joined Jack in conversation about what they termed the; Neighborhood Watch Patrol. Ed and Jack were key members. NWP watched over building sites for developers and recently began checking for garage doors being left open late at night. Last summer they worked with the Department of Natural Resources when a forest fire came close to Eagle Ridge by checking for hot spots. They kept watch 24/7 until the fire was no longer a threat. Guarding Boris would be the first time that normal surveillance of Eagle Ridge would be extended to an international figure. And, in addition, because they were anxious to use them, it gave each man the opportunity to use Nomadic 1000 outdoor waterproof walkie talkies.

Both men met early, seven a.m., in Ed's garage. Their carefully calculated plan began with Jack walking Dash, which included several passes by Boris's location on Pinehurst Drive. After two hours of walking, Jack and Dash were both ready to head home for a break. They were already one hour past Dash's normal routine. "Just once more, Dash. It's for our friend Boris." Dash stared at the lawn next to the sidewalk, walked over to a shaded area and laid down. Jack could only imagine what his amazing little Westie might be thinking. He'd proven to be more than a pet, and did possess a sixth sense. Dash also had something no other dog in the world had in America – Boris Yeltsin as a cuddle buddy. The thought made Jack smile. When Dash saw Jack smile the little canine lifted his head as if to signal, *okay, let's do this!* Dash walked over to Jack, looked up with a comforting look and proceeded to lead Jack on another pass down the block.

The sure-footed Westie and his owner turned on Eagle Ridge Drive and proceeded west two blocks past Pinehurst Drive when a slow-moving truck caught Jack's eye. Jack noticed a rental sticker on the back bumper from north of the border as Dash checked a nearby hydrant. He repeated the last four digits of the license plate to himself, because he was good at remembering numbers. The truck continued to drive to Whispering Pines Park at the other end of the boulevard, where it slowed and stopped. "Odd," Jack thought. The park was for residents only, but that rule was hard to enforce. The only exception would be if an out-of-state vehicle stopped. But even then, it was always nice to be hospitable. "Here we go," Jack said to himself, causing Dash to look up at his marathon walking owner.

The driver turned the engine off, but neither person moved until the passenger side window rolled down. Jack saw a hand then a spotting scope appeared. *What were they looking for?* The couple still hadn't made a move except for the scope. Jack radioed Ed of his location to let him know of the situation and that he was going to approach. Ed asked him if he needed assistance. "That's a negative, Ed. I'll be in contact." Ed sat in his car on the other side of Eagle Ridge about a half a mile away. He didn't feel comfortable just sitting and waiting, something inside said to go, now. Ed started the engine and headed for Whispering Pines Park.

Dash led Jack to the back of the truck with the leash fully extended to 20 feet. Jack saw that there were two people inside, a man and a woman. She held a map, but put it and the scope away as Jack walked up to the passenger side window.

§

Irina and Albert kept working their way, patiently, through the maze of streets that encompassed Eagle Ridge. Patience, a skill that had to be taught to most murderous natural born killers, almost kept Irina out of the assassin business. Eventually, she allowed the virtue of patience some consideration, which had proven, more than once, to be a life saver. Two years ago, she spent three days in a Cambodian jungle full of dangerous creatures, including her target, a rebel leader. She often thought of that time when she came to a crossroads in decision making – like now.

There were thirteen separate building phases that comprised Eagle Ridge, each with their own patterns of cul-de-sacs and meandering streets that confused even local visitors to the area. The posted community signs read: Eagle Ridge, Eagle Ridge Estates and a new development with most of the new construction called: Eagle Ridge Overlook. Albert considered himself to be a patient person in life, and especially when on assignment. He enjoyed hunting big game in the Scandinavian countries and had mounted trophies on his walls to prove his conquests. Taking down big game in those mountainous areas required a great deal of patience. However, given the enormity of the Yeltsin mission, he began to give into Irina's frustration, especially when the directions she'd been given did not match the sites they were driving through. "Where is the damn street, Albert?" "How would I know, Irina? You have the coordinates. "Look, we've both navigated through the bends and twists of Paris, Rome and Prague on separate occasions, we can do this." Irina looked tensely at her new partner and suppressed the urge to slit his throat, instead, she smiled and went through her notes one more time. They drove another two blocks when Irina realized where they were.

"Stop the truck, Albert." "What are you going to do, Comrade Dustakova, slit my throat?" Each shot hateful looks at the other. Irina finally pursed her lips and spoke softly. "We can figure this out, Albert, we've each also scouted our way through Saint Petersburg and Munich, we can damn well find Pinehurst Drive in Eagle Ridge!" She held the map closer to her face, hitting it in the middle to straighten it out, and was in the midst of studying it, when Albert noticed movement in the rearview mirror. "We may be in luck, my dear Irina." He turned to look through the back window, she in her side mirror, as both of them spotted a guy walking a dog, heading in their direction. "Would it be too much for you to ask for directions?" Albert slowly whispered. Irina immediately changed her facial expression from icy glare to that of a lovely stranger needing assistance. She flipped the visor down, checked her perfect teeth, full lips and *help us* expression, returned the visor in the upward position, winked at Albert, and slowly turned her head toward the passenger window.

Jack looked up in time to catch the woman's toothy smile. He continued to watch as she motioned for him to come closer. Dash alerted and turned into a twenty-pound stone, immovable, sensing danger. Jack on the other hand, seemed to be momentarily captivated by the stranger's waving motion. Before Jack could convince Dash that it was alright to move ahead, his phone rang. It was Fenton. The lady in the truck rolled the passenger side window down as Jack took the call, while holding his hand up signaling to her that he needed to take this call. She had a look of concern, and showed she understood by another wave of her hand.

"Hey, Jack, Fenton here." Jack could see from the caller ID who called, but decided not to make a smartass remark. "Fenton. Is there a problem?" "Heck, no, Jack. I understand you're taking the day off." Again, Jack had to hold back. "Can I call you back, Fenton, I'm in the middle of something." Just then Dash decided to bark as he continued to be on alert. "Oh, dog problems? Jack held the phone away from his ear and looked to the sky. When he brought it back to his face, he could hear his name being repeated over and over. "Yes, I'm here, Fenton." "Hey, I just wanted to give you a heads up.

The mayor wants to meet with you and your team as soon as possible. I'm calling to set an appointment." Jack made it quick. "Have Shelly call Jimmy and set a time for next week, yes, of course, next week then, bye." He hung up, preferring to talk to a lady needing help, rather than continue fencing with Fenton.

Jack stepped forward toward the truck as he put his phone away in his back pocket. "You could have taken your call, sir, we would have waited." She smiled at Jack who stood, transfixed like a statue. He felt like he'd been suddenly carbonized by the woman's radiant smile and foreign accent. Consequently, he found it difficult to put the phone away as he clumsily changed hands with the leash, in a failed attempt to keep a leaping Dash from jumping up on the truck side step.

Irina bent forward, showing some cleavage. "Cute dog, Westie, right?" Jack nodded, trying his best not to look at the woman's breasts. Meanwhile, the man in the driver's seat exited the truck and began to stretch.

"You look like you're new here. Is there something I can help you with, directions maybe?" The man came around the front of the truck as Ed drove past. Jack noticed and immediately felt instant relief, which is what Dash was also doing on one of the truck's tires. "Dash, back off, back, back." "Oh, that's okay, it isn't our truck," Albert offered, trying to catch himself as he said it. Irina shot him a look. Jack noticed the exchange, as Dash continued to sniff along the side of the truck.

"What I meant to say is, it's a rental." The man had a scar that ran from his left ear along the line of his chin to his mouth. That wasn't the only thing Jack noticed about the man, he also had an accent. One that Jack had recently heard before. In fact, so did the lady, slight, but it was there all the same. *These people have an accent – Russian?*

Albert, after making his comment about the truck, completed his stretching and returned to the vehicle in time for another icy stare from his partner. "Oh, sure, got it, a rental," Jack replied with a slight feeling of uneasiness. The driver seemed like he'd been driving a long time and the passenger appeared to be recently using a road map. Jack kept smiling, trying not to show his discomfort. Maybe some form of paranoia was starting to take over because of Boris. Jack felt a little better having Ed close by. He'd stopped his car along the curb on the other side of the street. The lady's question brought him out of his thoughts. "We could use some help Mister…?" "Templeman, Jack Templeman." Jack had to clear his throat in order to say his full name.

"We're trying to find an address: 2308 West Pinehurst Drive. Are we close?" Jack looked away as his face suddenly flushed having just heard the woman ask for Boris's address. *What the hell?* His mind raced with all kinds of thoughts, mostly – *what to do next?* Options, he and Ed had discussed a few scenarios, but not this. Jack managed lots of options at work, he knew how to get to the solution, if he had time, but the time was now. *Think, Jack.*

He turned back around facing the truck, furrowed his brow, looked down at the sidewalk, all the time trying not to pee himself like Dash was doing again on the tire. "Yes, ah, yes, I can help you with that. What was that address again?" Irina took a few seconds to study the man, who now looked nervous, standing in front of her. She slowly repeated the address, adding a smile that looked as though it would wear out any second.

Jack found his composure and provided the lady with directions. His explanation, which sounded complicated even to Jack, would take them the long way around the park first before making the turn onto Sterlingview Drive and then to Pinehurst. Jack needed time to warn Boris and Denis of the people looking for them. A bad feeling came over him in the form of paranoia. As the truck slowly drove off, Jack and Dash ran to Ed's car. Jack, out of breath and holding Dash, jumped into the car and shouted, "Boris's quick!" As the car sped off, Jack asked Ed if he brought the weapon they'd discussed, Ed's crossbow. Ed was a regional archery champion in high school and kept up with his love of the sport. He even hunted wild game with a bow and arrows. Jack never understood why, but now was not a time to question Ed about his sport of choice. "Great, at least it won't make much noise if you need to use it." Ed could tell that Jack was rattled as they pulled up to the house next door to 2308 West Pinehurst Drive.

Boris and Denis finished their final meeting with Bernard Jackson and one of his assistants. The pair would be leaving their temporary residence, a place that turned out to be a welcomed asylum, within hours. A number of logistical pieces had to fall into place in order to secure Yeltsin's safety. For one thing, once he began to leave, he had to keep moving steadily. There could be no hang ups or delays. For that reason, they had to wait just a few more hours. The Russians and the Americans involved in the mission felt better about a rendezvous happening later that evening. Two Suburbans would be arriving in four hours, promptly at nine. They would join Bernard Jackson and his crew in making sure President Yeltsin traveled secretly and safely, without any notice, out of Spokane and on to Moscow. For the time being, Boris and Denis waited. The last few hours would be spent packing their few belongings and maintaining watch for any possible interruptions in the schedule.

Boris looked forward to seeing his family and getting back to work as President of his beloved Russia. Even though the escape had been deemed necessary by both governments involved, the time away had been unsettling for both Boris and Denis, who also longed to catch up with his family, holding his wife in his arms and hugging his three children. "There was a time in this place when I thought I'd go crazy. But that didn't happen. I have to give Jack Templeman credit for that," Boris said with a big smile on his face as shared his thoughts with his most trusted comrade.

"And, so, it wasn't my cooking that saved you from craziness?" Denis added with a laugh. The laughter had a nervous air to it. "What is there to do sometimes, but laugh my friend." Boris offered as he admitted that Denis's meals were better than he had expected, but Jack gave me something I had forgotten." Boris didn't have time to elaborate, instead he stopped talking and pointed at a shadow that appeared on the other side of the slider.

Denis gently put a hand on Boris's shoulder and pushed him down behind the sofa. "Stay there and don't move, sir." Denis held his handgun out in front of him as he made his way to the window adjacent to the slider. Pulling the curtain back gently, he looked down to see Dash looking back at him. Jack was crouched in a nearby window well. Ed was pressed up against the house holding a crossbow and wearing a quiver loaded with smaller arrows called bolts made to fit in crossbows.

Denis knocked on the window and motioned for Jack and Ed to come in through the slider. The two men rushed in, Ed nearly poking Denis in the eye with a bolt. Both were out of breath, Jack spoke first, while Ed looked out the back window. "I just gave directions to two people I've never seen before." "Directions, Jack?" Denis's look reminded Jack to finish his thought. "Oh, I mean directions to this address." "Is that bad, this house is still technically on the market, Jack." Denis was right. "Yes, but there's something fishy about these people. Even Dash picked up on their Russian accents."

Boris and Dash were going at it. The big guy had the little dog down on the rug playing with a towel, swinging the dog back and forth. "If Dash is upset, so am I," Boris claimed as he ran down the hall with Dash close behind nipping at his heels. Jack admitted he might be jumping to conclusions. "Hey, they could be looking to buy, I guess." Jack sounded as if he was trying to convince himself.

Meanwhile, Ed changed positions and stood by the front window, watching for the rental truck they'd seen at the park. Boris came into the kitchen where Denis busied himself making sandwiches. "Look, I think maybe your conclusions are jumping all over the place, Jack. Why don't you and Ed stick around and wait with us for a while. Both of you are good company and we can shoot some breeze and hope nobody is shooting anything else at us." Boris looked up, hoping to get a laugh. "You know I am making joke, right?" Smiles slowly began to appear. It became evident to Jack that Boris was attempting to lighten the tension in the room.

They were beginning to relax when the doorbell rang. Everyone froze. Denis was the first to thaw as Ed pulled back a corner of the front curtain. "It's Ellen."

§

The sun would soon set and they were behind schedule. Albert, clearly agitated, had been driving long enough around the Eagle place that it seemed more and more like an unforgiving maze. Albert was ready to shoot someone and that did not bode well for anybody, especially his partner, Irina. "What the hell, Irina? This is ridiculous."

"Time to calm yourself, darling, for God's sake. Take deep breath – or two." Her sassy reply didn't help the situation. No one likes to be told to calm themselves, especially an international assassin doing his superior a favor because he, Albert, happened to be in the wrong place at the wrong time.

Albert had just completed his 15th mission in 12 months. He needed some space and had been promised some time off by his superiors. Once the approval came in, for two weeks, he boarded the flight to Vancouver, British Columbia where he rented a truck and drove to Jasper, Alberta to visit a retired military colleague and to do some hunting. Albert barely had time to unpack when he received the call to join Irina, his fellow assassin, in Nelson, B.C. So much for down time and enjoying his favorite pastime. He had to remind himself that what he did for a living, which was very lucrative, superseded his personal life. Attempting to take time away from the contractual killing of strangers always had been a challenging lifestyle. It became clear that his life centered around one action - hunting.

"You will enjoy this one, Albert." His boss's voice even changed into a soft whisper as he'd said it. After a brief explanation over a secured line, Albert knew that this new mission could be the pinnacle of his twenty-year career. Killing Boris Yeltsin would not only give him prestige, it would please people on both sides of the political spectrum. Those who supported Yeltsin politically, but were concerned about his recent inability to control inflation. And those who hated his injection of a capitalistic ideology into a Communistic society. As his boss put it: "Yeltsin is unique, you either hate him, because he is not a true communist, or you despise him because he is a failing Russian leader. Most people affected by his leadership didn't really understand how the man was promoted into office, let alone how Russia would end up under his rule."

Albert could have used the down time, but the more his boss spoke, the more enticing the job became. Albert cut his hunting plans short and was on the road within the hour.

Irina looked over at her cohort as they slowed to a stop next to an empty lot. She knew they would find their target - she always did. Her mind had a different kind of chatter happening. The sunshine glare through the windshield caused her to close her eyes as she took a second to float into a memory. As a Red Sparrow graduate, she'd often escape a terrible situation by willfully transcending into a better place. She now thought of a Swiss assignment that nearly resulted in her death. He was handsome, rich, and very good in bed. He made her feel sexy and asked for her hand in marriage, which caused Irina to question her occupation for a short time. That momentary lapse allowed her target time to figure out what was really happening in the moment. Irina felt out of control for the first time in her life. How could she? How could she take his life? By the time she recovered, the man had a knife at her throat. If it hadn't been for her handler, she would have died. The result of her inaction came quick, she was sent back to Moscow for "re-education," which nearly killed her a second time.

Snapping out of her daydream, Irina came to the same conclusion she did in order to find the Swiss banker hunk, and watching as a blade cut into his wonderfully romantic heart. She looked at Albert, who had said something to her, she could tell because his mouth was moving. She did not hear what was said. She'd been caught up in thought.

"Take a deep breath." Albert continued to stare, so she repeated herself. They both took a deep breath and as Irina opened her eyes, a smile appeared. She pursed her lips and agreed that the man with the dog, Jack, had sent them in the wrong direction. Why? They went back over the directions they'd been given and within a matter of minutes located Pinehurst Drive. "Park here. Let's walk." She could see by the addresses that they were close to the target's residence, Irina could feel it. Her instincts and intuition never let her down. They were her hidden assets that she had learned to use as a Sparrow. Shadows were coming on as the sun began to set. Darkness would be arriving soon and they would use that darkness to their advantage. Bad things happen in the dark, and that thought nearly took her breath away.

"No, let's not park here. We'll drive the truck back down the hill to the rock quarry we passed on the way into Eagle Ridge." Albert expertly backed the truck behind a stand of trees after finding the seldom used service road. Irina was impressed and told him so. The truck would be used in their escape. They unpacked their weapons and ordinance required to complete their mission. The two made the trek back up the hill, through the park, and back onto the streets, looking like they'd just taken a healthy hike toting two full backpacks.

Albert's custom designed eighty-pound backpack contained everything a veteran assassin required; night vision goggles, two automatic handguns with silencers, a long-range collapsible sniper rifle, ammo magazines, twelve-inch knife, rations and gloves. It also housed a small flask of his favorite scotch that he carried all over the world. Irina walked next to him carrying a six-inch stiletto knife with a serrated edge in her belt – a precious weapon of choice, and sporting a slightly smaller backpack. They didn't look out of place because they were trained to fit in anywhere.

The hills, valley, and creek around Eagle Ridge reminded them of European countries they'd operated in, mostly France. Between the two of them, Albert was more the outdoor type. He owned a cottage that overlooked the Mecklenburg Lake canal. The area has a global reputation for hunting and fishing. Albert spent the majority of his off time with a small group of friends hunting red deer. He thought of those times as they drove past Deer Park on their way to Spokane earlier in the day. For all intents and purposes, Irina and Albert were very comfortable with their progress so far. They took great pride in blending in wherever they worked. They even held hands as they strolled along the sidewalk, smiling at one another as if returning from a hike, much like the woman, with a quick stride, thirty feet ahead of them. As the woman turned and began walking up to the front door of a house on Pinehurst Drive, the assassins crossed the street, disappearing into a small forested area.

"2308 Pinehurst Drive. Cut across, into that field," Irina suddenly directed him. Albert moved swiftly as Irina led the way. The area was well-groomed with a thick grove of pine trees that they settled into, facing the front of their target's house. Their movements were quick, cat-like, but not unnoticeable to the trained, or in this case, nosey eyes of a neighbor.

Fred Brewster happened to be taking out the garbage at the same time the two new faces entered the trees on the vacant lot next to his property. Fred would normally have waved or said hello, but they moved too fast. He knew everyone, but the setting sun cast shadows on the unfamiliar couple. He would watch for them in the future with the hope of meeting his new neighbors, if, in fact, that's who they were. Fred made a mental note that he hoped to God he would remember as he turned to go into the house and watch the news with his wife. Watching the news every night at 5:30pm was their thing. He especially liked old…what's his name? Tom somebody on NBC.

The door to 2308 opened and the woman who had been walking ahead of them entered the house. If that happened to be where Boris Yeltsin had been staying, it defied logic, according to what Albert and Irina now felt. "What's going on? Our informant better be right." Albert had the reputation for being meticulous. He watched the house through a spotting scope for more activity – Irina called in their contact to let him know of their location.

§

"Ellen, what are you doing here?" Jack was truly surprised and concerned at the same time. Dash flew to Ellen out of Boris's arms as everyone stood looking at one another. Ellen had a stunned look on her face. She knew two of the four men in the room, but the other two gentlemen were complete strangers, except the big guy. *Could it be? No, that's not…*

She blindly reached for and hugged her husband and stood looking at the man authorities everywhere were looking for – worldwide. Ellen made her way into the former Miller residence. Not much had changed, except for the used furniture. Ellen knew the layout of the house like the back of her hand, having visited Georgia Miller over the years. Ellen didn't have to worry about stepping around the living room while her frozen gaze locked on to the face of the President of Russia. "THE Boris Yeltsin? Here... in Spokane?" Boris smiled and turned his head slightly. The petite pretty lady was right, and frankly, her recognition made him feel some relief. He held his smile as he walked her direction. Jack stood mumbling some excuse for not telling her before as Boris reached out to greet Ellen. He gently wrapped his big fists around her hands and leaning forward said, "Busted," which made Denis smile because the American term came so naturally from the man. Everyone in the room began to laugh, one at a time, which became contagious as each person joined in, with Ellen being the last as she excitedly shook the man's hands.

Without looking at him, Ellen spoke when the laughter subsided. "Jack, this man, the President of Russia, is your chess partner?" The laughter came again. And when it stopped, so did the tension in the room.

"I was a little worried, Jack. You went for a walk with Dash, remember? And then Janice called asking if I'd seen Ed. What are you two, teenagers?" When she said that, Boris chuckled out loud. "I'm sorry, Ellen, excuse, please, for laughing. But that's funny, Jack acting like – teenager." Ellen let his comment pass and turned to Ed. "Ed, you need to call Janice." Ed excused himself and made the call.

Across the street, Fred Brewster was busy trying to find his glasses. "I know I left them somewhere around here." Amy overheard from the kitchen where she was busy fixing dinner. "They're here in the kitchen, Fred." Amy wished she had a dollar for every time she found his glasses for him. She was in the middle of sharing that thought with Fred when there was a knock at the back door. Without looking, Fred opened the door to two people dressed in black, wearing masks. What happened next came in a blur. Fred and Amy were told to cooperate if they wanted to live. The words came quickly in whispered broken English. Fred and Amy looked at one another as they were placed, back-to-back, on dining room chairs, and tied up with duct tape. The room went silent as the two intruders set up in the living room, facing the front door of the house across the street.

Fred felt guilty for not checking to see who knocked before opening the back door. The house hadn't been this silent since Amy had to stay with a sick relative for a week last year. Strangely, the silence added to the tension. *What to do?* Fred squinted in order to see one of the intruders looking out their front window. *And what's going on across the street?* he thought to himself. Fred's mind wouldn't shut off as Amy began to hum Amazing Grace.

*Chapter 9*

## GROCERY STORE PARKING LOT - CHENEY/ SPOKANE ROAD

Bernard Jackson coordinated the timing on the Yeltsin pickup. He'd been counting the days, seventeen to be exact, until they'd be able to complete the mission. The black suburban sat idling in a grocery store parking lot about a mile away, below Eagle Ridge, waiting for the rendezvous with two other bullet-proof Suburbans that would complete the caravan. Seventy- millimeter high-powered machine guns and six additional, Secret Service officers would be embedded in those vehicles. They'd just made their last pass by the Yeltsin residence or *hideout* as Jackson thought of it. Jackson's watch showed 7pm, two hours to go and all would be well. Jackson knew his planning would be nothing but perfection. He took great pride in his work and his allegiance to a better world.

§

Albert checked the duct tape on both hostages as Irina used the spotting scope to check the residence across the street. In a low mumbled tone, Irina spoke as she scoped, "We need to confirm that Yeltsin is in that residence, Albert." He handed Irina the headset after setting up the portable long-distance microphone. He fit the pieces of the listening device together. It looked like a pool cue with the directional receiver at the tip. Once in place, and earphones attached, Irina listened. It took her only a minute or two before she motioned to Albert that she had something. Her head moved as if being told what position to turn, but in reality, she found the conversation engaging, even funny at one point. Then her eyes widened, she put her hand on Albert's shoulder as a seductive expression appeared on her face. "He's there. And he's so... busted." She looked at Albert after having said what she heard in a loud whisper. Albert just shrugged his shoulders and wrinkled his brow.

Fred Brewster heard every word they said. His eyes may have been failing over the years, but not his ears. *Did they just mention Boris Yeltsin's name, living in the old Miller place across the street?*

The two assassins had a plan that had been discussed, but not rehearsed. A few minutes later they left the Brewsters' darkened home, looking like a couple in the community out for a stroll. The only difference between these two and everyone else that lived in this pristine, quiet, development, was the fact that Irina and Albert were on a mission to kill.

§

"Ah, uh, guys, two people are coming up the walk." After Ed's announcement there was a lot of shuffling. Jack took a turn looking out the window. Sure enough, it was them, he recognized the woman first. Jack looked at Denis. "I have a bad feeling about this," he stated emphatically. Denis told him that Jackson and his men would be arriving in two hours. "Can't wait. We have to get out of here," was Jack's response.

The doorbell rang as five people and a dog exited out the back slider. Jack led the way and Ed brought up the rear. Boris was in no shape to be running, rolling behind bushes and hiding, but he followed as best he could. Denis checked his gun as he positioned himself behind Boris. It had been about a year since he'd actually been in the field. Driving the limo and fixing meals had added some weight to his large frame that appeared to be counterproductive at that moment.

The group managed to stay together under Jack's guidance. Afterall, he knew this area better than anyone, with the exception of Ed. The site plans for the area had been on his drawing board at work for nearly two years. Random street lights helped guide their way as the small group jogged through low brush, behind new homes under construction.

§

Irina stood on the front porch, unscrewing the front porch light, as Albert circled around to the back of the house. Having recently celebrated his fortieth, he prided himself on being able to move swiftly while carrying a heavy load on his back. His birthday celebration took place in Prague, the capital of the Czech Republic. His grandmother lived in the Old Town area and hosted the party for him. Albert wasn't one to reminisce, but an email he received earlier in the day notified him of her unexpected death. *Focus Albert*, he thought to himself. He slowly made his way toward the back slider. The room was dark, in fact the whole house looked unoccupied, though Irina had heard people inside just minutes before. He reached for the door handle and tried the slider, it slid back without a sound, nice and smooth.

He felt as though no one was there, but had to check to make sure. Albert turned on instinct and surveyed the backyard and the land beyond. Through his night vision goggles he saw a line of people making their way up the other side of a small hill, beyond the back fence, heading away from the house. He flipped the goggles up and swiftly moved through the kitchen area, gun in hand, heading for the front door. "What took so long?" Irina didn't appreciate waiting in the dark after unscrewing the porch light. Albert motioned for her to follow as he pointed out back. "Put on your goggles, look." He pointed to what looked like a stream of green figures making their way up the side of a hill and out of sight. Irina gave the command, "Let's go."

§

Jack led the group around the outside of a house that had just been framed-in. The walls were up and the roof was on, but not much more construction. "Be... be careful, there could be holes in the f...floor. Everyone, including Jack, were trying to catch their breath. "Ed, keep eyes on the Miller's old place, while we take a minute." They rested, sitting on a long stack of two by fours, each person thankful for stopping. "I will cover this position if you want to keep going." Denis's suggestion made sense to Jack, but they didn't know for sure who or how many people may be following them and Denis staying behind would leave Boris without his bodyguard. "Denis, you should stay with Boris for now." Denis agreed then shouted, "Look, I see movement crossing through the back fence where we started, Jack." There happened to be just enough street light for Jack and Denis to confirm movement.

Jack's group held their position that was approximately six blocks from Jack and Ellen's house and one block from Whispering Pines Park. Jack and Ed quickly made a plan. Ed would stay behind, covering the others from the rear. "We'll head for the park and from there to our house." Everyone nodded. Ellen looked scared as she gave Ed a quick hug.

Taking control of the situation felt good to Jack. That nagging feeling of added, unexpected, responsibility suddenly appealed to him. Jack, Ellen, Boris and Denis left with Dash running full leash. Jack told Ed not to take any unnecessary chances, but what did that mean exactly?

Ed La Drew had more than a dozen shiny trophies proclaiming his achievements in archery. He'd told Jack that, even in the evening, with his crossbow he could hit a target at two hundred feet with minimum light. Since the street lights were brighter around the park perimeter, Ed felt he had no problem seeing a target. If he had to take someone down, he'd do it. It never occurred to him that one day he would actually be in a position to shoot a person. Ed turned on his headlamp and moved upstairs into the partially completed house. He had to be careful not to shine the light for very long, but he had to get his bearings. The shell of a house had been left clean that day, thankfully. Straight ahead, not far from the front door, were steps leading up a staircase. One problem though, there was no hand rail, not to mention a few steps missing, the partially completed floor, which had its challenges. Once he reached the steps, Ed had to watch each step, one wrong move could send him back downstairs, fast. Ed made it to the top in good shape and began to crab-walk with his head down. He wanted to look out to the park where Jack was leading the group. When he reached a west facing wall, he discovered one large window frame. He immediately turned his light out. Ed could see the park and Jack's small group heading across an open grassy area about the size of a football field, a wide-open view.

"Footsteps." Ed whispered to himself. There was someone else in the house. His heart jumped into his throat. Ed slowly reached into his quiver for a bolt, placed it in the slot of the crossbow and froze. He could hear more movement directly below. He turned from the window to face the stairs he'd just came from and froze once again. He took a deep breath, let it out slowly, checked the bow, and waited to fire off a shot.

§

Irina motioned Albert forward into the unfinished home. She waited patiently while he checked the place out. The area sat silent on a hill overlooking a park with ornamental street lights lining a large field of semi-circled grass. She favored her mountain log hideaway in the Bavarian Alps, but this one had potential. Off in the distance she heard voices coming from the park two blocks away. She snapped back, out of her home critique, just in time. Out of nowhere, a small dog came charging down the street toward the house – barking. Someone running behind yelling for the dog to stop. Mash, Stash, strange name, no, "Dash," a man's voice called out from beyond.

The stairs creaked as the assassin proceeded to make his way up. Albert noticed that the stairs were not finished, no railing, open on both sides. Ed moved in behind two large pieces of wall board. Shuffling across the floor, trying not to make a sound, caused Ed's eyes to water. He felt like sneezing. As he held his right forefinger under his nose, he saw the top of someone's head begin to rise above the floor. Ed slowly moved his hand back on the trigger. He then heard a faint whisper as the head disappeared. "Forget it, I'm not doing this," Albert said quietly to himself and turned around. As Albert descended, Ed came out from behind the wall board with a bolt fitted on his crossbow ready to fire. Albert had to watch his step outside as he joined Irina and gave her the all clear for the house. Irina flipped her goggles up and asked, "Did you hear the dog?"

"Yes. It sounded like the mutt we heard in the park with that guy."

"Follow the mutt, Albert. Who knows, we might get lucky. Go."

The little dog suddenly turned as if to lead the two assassins to their prey. Jack waited for Dash on the curb by the park, knowing that the dog probably smelled trouble or thoughts of Ed had been forgotten. Jack could see a light flashing in the house behind Dash as he ran and jumped into Jack's waiting arms. The chase was on. Jack ran faster than he thought possible. He ducked down behind some greenery. "You've gained weight, Dash." Jack had to catch his breath.

After counting to ten, he and Dash came out of the hedge they'd been hiding behind, like being shot from a cannon.

Jack could feel Dash tense up as the hairy little hound looked back over Jack's shoulder. Although he wasn't used to running with the dog in his arms, Jack kicked his pace into as much overdrive as he could muster. He could feel there were people behind, like ghosts in the cemetery on Halloween. He also felt his thighs and lower back begin to tighten up. You had to believe in times like this, even though you didn't want to, but you had to in order to survive. Run!

§

"Dash, go home, no, bad dog, Ed whispered to himself as he watched Jack and Dash make a run for it." *Go guys*. Ed couldn't believe the little dog turned back as if he'd heard Ed's whisper. He watched as Jack scooped up the dog and ran with him in his arms, heading for the forested area behind the amphitheater on the far side of the park. Westies aren't huge dogs, but they are solid and do pack some weight.

Ed went for his crossbow, leveled it and stood up. Two shapes were gaining on Jack as Dash began to bark out a warning. The streetlight revealed a silhouette of an object that looked like a gun. "Jesus, Jack, run." Ed almost yelled as he aimed his crossbow at the person holding what had to be a gun pointed at his friend. The archer snapped off a quick shot, which missed to the left of the target. Ed could tell because there were sparks from the bolt tip as it hit the asphalt. "Okay, more rise and to the right," he said to himself as he quickly reloaded. Ed took another deep breath knowing he had to hurry, blinked his watery eyes and slowly squeezed the trigger. A moment later – "Bullseye, you bastard." The person stopped aiming toward Jack and collapsed, knees first, on the ground. Ed took a third deep breath, exhaled slowly, watching his target as he prepared for his next shot. "Run Jack."

§

"Arrggh, robho, I've been hit." Albert cried out as Irina leveled her silenced gun and fired twice at the man disappearing with a dog. The nearly noiseless shots sounded like phew, phew. "I think I hit him." Irina smiled as she holstered her pistol and turned her attention to Albert who scrambled behind a hedge. He held an arrow that protruded from his shoulder. "People told me that you normally have a stick up your ass, Albert, I never expected it to move all the way up to the shoulder." Clearly the man did not appreciate her poor attempt at humor. Albert thought about responding, but changed his mind. Instead, he shifted his pack strap to his right side having been shot in the upper left shoulder. He'd been wounded more than once over the last twenty years, and made light of the fact that there appeared to be an archer living in this community. "The shot wasn't that good. I'm still here." His comment fell on deaf ears.

It concerned them that the archer's shot had come from behind. "You circle back and take care of the situation. I'll keep moving after them. Yeltsin's got to be with the group ahead." Albert tried to break off part of the bolt as he turned back to the unfinished house. His attempt to break off the carbon fiber stick only caused more pain. "Arrggh." After a fit of swearing, Albert determined that the archer had to be positioned upstairs in the house he failed to clear earlier. "Arrggh." The angle of the shot proved that it had have come from that half-constructed house. As Albert headed back, Irina moved like a cat chasing a mouse, replicating the same route that Jack had taken moments earlier.

No sooner had she begun to run into the open grassy field of the park, than two more bolts came raining down close by, one narrowly missing the feline-like assassin by a foot and embedding itself in the trunk of a tree. "I'm going to kill that arrow flinging bastard." Albert snorted under his breath as he spotted the crossbow protruding from the unfinished upper floor window. It was his fault he literally hadn't taken the extra steps to ensure their safety earlier. He would correct that and return to Irina to complete their mission. Behind him, Irina continued over the open area, which eventually led her into a stand of pine trees, where the man and dog had disappeared.

Ed saw the man heading back his way. He had eight more bolts and knew how to use them. Could he make a stand against this person? A crossbow versus a gun? The question didn't linger, Ed knew what he had to do.

Albert had the advantage. He just needed a clear shot. All of a sudden, his opportunity took flight. Night vision showed the man running from the house. The archer had been lucky up to this point, but that was about to change as Albert set his sights on the figure running across the open field. He had a silencer, no one but the target would know. He took the shot, the figure fell. Albert turned and winced and began to jog back to Irina. His shoulder hurt like hell as he radioed that he needed her coordinates.

§

Jack couldn't go another step. The feeling of exhaustion superseded his need to run at that moment. He had just entered the woods and stopped right in his tracks. Jack looked around for the others, still cradling Dash in his arms. He couldn't remember the last time he had been chased, let alone dodging bullets. He felt lucky Dash was okay and that they were safe for now. Dash began to wiggle out of Jack's hold. His furry friend noticed them first. "Who is it, Dash?" The moment Jack saw Ellen he let Dash go. The ball of white fur ran for Ellen just as Jack felt a stinging pain in his right arm, near his bicep. In one motion, Ellen handed Dash's leash to Boris and rushed to Jack's side. He had fallen, as if hit by one of the shots, and rolled through some brush and into a slight depression behind a large boulder. "Jack, where's the wound?" "Ugh, yes. My arm. Where's Boris and Denis?" "Waiting over there." Ellen pointed to a stack of wood recently cut from a couple of pine trees that had been cleared from some power lines. A troop of Boy Scouts helped stack the wood as part of a community clean program after a recent storm. The neatly placed logs were sawed in four-foot lengths and piled six feet high. The stack provided enough protection for the entire group who had gathered behind it for temporary safety. After a quick check of Jack's arm, Ellen was relieved to find only a long surface scratch showing through his ripped open his jacket. She tied her scarf over the wound to stop the bleeding and helped Jack to his feet.

Denis had his gun drawn as the two ran up. Boris stood and asked: "Are you alright, my friend? We saw what happened." "I'll be okay, but the people looking for you are close behind." Ellen suggested they call the police, but Boris disagreed. Ellen questioned his decision. Jack interrupted. "We don't have much time, but Boris is right. The cops would just get in the way, call your CIA contact. Let's head to our house, I'll explain." No one questioned Jack's suggestion. Denis saw movement heading their way and stayed behind to provide cover. As the group headed for Jack and Ellen's, three blocks from the forested area Denis took cover and leveled his gun. Four shots rang out, fired in quick succession, from Denis's gun. Seeing no movement, Denis then sprinted off behind the group. They hoped to lose the attackers along the way, giving them time to contact the Federal authorities and arrange for Boris and Denis's safe departure.

§

Fred Brewster normally enjoys Amy's singing, especially in church as a member of Saint Martin's choir. Amy had the voice of an angel, with numerous awards and had won the Song Bird of the Northwest Award four times. A highly regarded prize that Amy intended on competing for, once again, later in the year. But humming was another matter. After nearly one hundred renditions of "Amazing Grace" hummed through duct tape, Fred had had it. But what to do? His mind, already cluttered with thoughts of the terrifying home invasion that interrupted their weekly meatloaf dinner, Fred's favorite meal, they now had to deal with how to free themselves. The emotion of it all had to be overwhelming, especially on an empty stomach. The intruders had not returned and Fred had more than one question about what might be happening on their block. He made a mental note to cause quite a stir at the next HOA meeting.

Thoughts kept racing through his head along with another rendition of "Amazing Grace." *Who were those two men that had been staying across the street for the last few weeks?* They seemed friendly enough, even though they said very little. The times Fred happened to walk outside, as they passed by, he received hearty smiles and waves, but not much else. Their communication involved mostly a friendly hello, and a reminder of what a nice day it happened to be at the moment. Nothing more. Fred remembered discussing the men's accents with Amy last week. He found it odd that the two men suddenly showed up, foreigners really, from out of nowhere. Between their accents and that funny looking mustache on the bigger man, one couldn't help but be suspicious. Fast forward to what happened this evening. And now here they sat, wrapped up tight, like two poorly sealed presents under the tree at Christmas. Something had to be done.

The two invaders were gone, obviously chasing after the suspected gents from across the street. Fred tried to calm himself, but to no avail. He suffered from high blood pressure, and learned how to breathe deep to calm himself. And so, he began. At first, he tried to time his breathing in unison with Amy's humming. That worked for a short time until his breathing and her humming became almost combative as if in competition with one another. Additionally, Fred's lips were dry. When he went to lick them some of the duct tape adhesive rubbed off on his tongue, which reminded him of the time Amy asked him to lick 103 Christmas envelopes. The thought gave him a headache.

The pressure to do something about their potential demise and what might be happening in their community, kept building inside until his left eye lid began to twitch, a sure sign that his blood pressure was rising to an unsafe level.

His mind raced from one thing to another, finally settling on how their secluded Eagle Ridge might be changing. The Brewster's moved to Spokane from Los Angeles, ten years earlier, after Fred retired from the police force. He'd spent the last fifteen of his thirty years as a homicide detective. All they wanted was a nice, quiet place to retire. If Amy could talk, which she couldn't, she'd most likely tell Fred to settle down and let the Lord take care of things. Fred's relationship with the Lord included a little more practical thinking than faith, especially in times like this.

It didn't take him long to hatch a plan. At 66 years of age, he felt he couldn't wait on the Lord. He had to somehow get to the kitchen, find a knife, and free them. His captors had used plenty of duct tape, nearly the whole silver colored roll, wrapped around and around from head to toe including their newly recovered dining room chairs. Fred knew the tape would leave marks on each of them and the chairs, but would loosen with movement. He wasn't sure if his chair could be moved easily, but he had to try.

With more determination than he had ever felt before, Fred began to rock the chair. Slowly at first, then progressively faster in a syncopated rhythm. Ironically, his rocking motion, inadvertently, caused Amy to think that her Fred was really getting into her humming. *Amen to that, Freddy.* So, Amy gladly upped the ante and began to hum even louder, which was an unwelcome surprise to her already flustered husband. Fred couldn't share his feelings because of the duct tape covering his mouth. His pleas for her to stop sounded to Amy as though he'd begun to hum along to the song that gave her so much solace in this time of sorrow. If he could, Fred would have shared his plan, but he couldn't, so he increased his rocking motion, causing Amy to take her humming up a notch. The sudden collaboration of the two dining room chairs swaying to the droning hum of "Amazing Grace" moved Amy to tears. The stream of water coming down her cheeks helped to loosen the top part of the tape on her mouth, causing her hum to become more of a kazoo sound, enhancing the vibrato of her hum. That change in pitch moved her to the highest spiritual level she'd ever known. The humming vibrations matched the stuttered movement of Fred's chair as he steadily headed toward the kitchen. Amy nearly hyperventilated before figuring out what Fred's intentions were as she caught sight of him nearing the kitchen. She felt relief begin to flow over her as she began to reduce her hum, which oddly caused more of a flapping in her lips. The sound Amy now emitted could have been mistaken for intoxication rather than something spiritually inspired. The last thing she remembered before passing out was her Freddy standing over her with a knife.

§

With the wave of his gloved hand, Bernard Jackson gave the signal for the three black Suburbans; Alpha, in the lead, Beta, in the middle, and Delta, the last in the caravan, to move out. Jackson's heavily armored Suburban, Delta, had a Browning fifty caliber machine gun mounted in the back, which meant they would be responsible for covering the rear flank. New intelligence revealed that a Russian faction, known to support Putin, may make an attempt to kill Yeltsin before his return. Although Yeltsin's supporters had reclaimed control in Russia, there were pockets of anti-government fighters loyal to his political rivals.

As the caravan snaked out of the parking lot and along the old Inland Empire Highway, heading to Eagle Ridge and Pinehurst Drive for the last time, each person in the twelve-man team remained on high alert. Rescuing Yeltsin, seventeen days ago, had been a coup. Returning him, unharmed, had the potential of being an even more dangerous matter. As the government team pulled up to the Pinehurst residence, Jackson noticed the front porch light out and the door ajar. He adjusted his headset and announced: "Sargent, deploy four men from Alpha and Beta to surround the house." As the four made their way to the four corners of the house, Jackson and his driver made their way to the front door, guns drawn. From behind, Jackson heard a commotion. When he turned, there was an older man being taken to the ground in the front yard. He was covered in duct tape.

"Boy that didn't take you guys long to get here." Fred left his wife laying on the couch in their front room when he saw the authorities pull up. Amy would have joined Fred, but beyond being exhausted from her humming, she collapsed on their couch and was stuck to the upholstery. Fred had a similar problem in that he'd spent 20 minutes trying to remove his duct tape without loss of hair and skin. "I have to remember to get more of this stuff," he reminded himself as an official approached wearing a blue windbreaker with CIA in gold letters on the front.

"Who are *you* sir, and what's going on?"

"That's a question for you, not me. I'm a taxpaying citizen wanting to know what the heck is happening in our neighborhood?" Fred replied sternly.

Fred, quickly as he could, told Jackson what had just

occurred across the street to him and his wife. Immediately, the Government team sprang into action. They were in the midst of clearing the Pinehurst house when shouting and muffled shots rang out from the park nearby.

§

Jack led the group through the Templeman's side yard along a flagstone path under a pergola and in through the back door. Ellen had left the house with only one lamp left on, the place was basically dark as they walked into the kitchen. "Keep the lights off, El, let's head to the garage and make the exchange with Jackson's team there."

"Even in darkness you have nice house, Jack. Ellen, you must be responsible, am I right?" Ellen's smile at Boris was lost in the darkness as Jack hurried everyone into the garage, thinking they could make the exchange before the attackers discovered their whereabouts. "Denis, call Jackson. Tell him to make pick up here, at Jack's house." Boris sounded official. It came easily to him, shifting from casual to Presidential, that's what people liked about the man.

Jack gave Denis the address, a second later two shots came through the garage window above the workbench. Ellen screamed as they all scrambled behind "Old Blue", Jack's '82 Ford pickup truck, parked facing out toward the second garage door. Jack could have sold the old dependable workhorse, making Ellen happy, but the truck came in handy for hauling and odd jobs. Ellen considered it an eye sore and the HOA asked Jack not to park it in the driveway. Jack loved the truck, but understood Ellen's concern, especially when the color began to oxidize. Denis moved closer to Jack with his gun out. "They have eyes on us, don't move, I will return fire."

Sirens could be heard in the distance intermixed with the sound of gunfire and the intermittent thud of bullets hitting the house. Denis made his way to the workbench, to the side of the broken garage window. He immediately began returning fire in the direction of flashes coming from a community park area across from Jack and Ellen's.

§

Irina had had it. Yeltsin, and the people helping him, must die soon or she would start shooting anything that moved. She called Albert. "Where are you?" "I'm here, I see you," Albert responded out-of-breath. Seeing that he had her flank, she positioned herself 50 meters across from the blown-out garage window, and for an instant, had a clear shot at two individuals, one had to be Yeltsin. She fired off several rounds and signaled for Albert to launch his RPG at the larger garage door. It took him less than a minute, but eventually Albert held the weapon outward and waited for her signal. Irina watched to see if any neighbors were brave enough to come out of hiding with a weapon before firing off the big blast.

"What was she waiting for?" Albert felt his nerves begin to dance, causing a smile to slowly appear as siren sounds drew closer. The smile slipped away as a crossbow bolt hit him square in the center of his back. "Bastard. I… chased him… away." Albert still held the launcher, but found it much harder to aim. Slowly he slumped to the ground, his vision beginning to blur as he saw Irina, signaling a go to launch the grenade. Albert pulled the trigger of the RPG, but instead of the grenade hitting the garage door square in the middle, as intended, it hit the cornice of the house above the door. The explosion was the last Albert would ever witness.

Irina doubled over in shock. She was more disappointed with the fact that Albert missed his target than about what had happened to the famed assassin. She slipped behind a small rock wall, shielding her from returning gunfire coming from the garage and providing her with a few moments to consider her next move. Neighbors began emerging outside. Shouts of "What's happening?" and "Go back inside," echoed through the cul-de-sac.

With Albert eliminated, Irina decided to pull the plug on the operation and retreat. She had two concerns; The oncoming sirens and the person firing the arrows. *The archer is good. Poor Albert.* She'd been able to escape from more dramatic situations before and she was determined to make it happen again. Besides, who knows what happened to the people inside that garage when the RPG hit. Hopefully, there were casualties.

Irina moved like a cat as she retraced the path that led to her current location. It didn't take long for her to find the forested tree line leading down the hill, away from Eagle Ridge Estates into Eagle Ridge Overlook. It had been Albert's idea to hide the truck in the rock quarry about a quarter mile away. Irina made sure she had the duplicate set of keys as her dark figure disappeared into the woods.

Irina had to be careful as she slipped and slid her way along a small animal path that appeared out of nowhere. She made a sharp turn when she ran into a low hanging branch that threw her off the path and into a patch of Canadian Thistle. She rolled through the sharp sting of the thistle, landing on a hard surface of rock boulders. "Damn." She was thankful that her backpack worked as a shield and took most of the impact. The woman's resolve to escape showed as she jumped up and kept going. She told herself that she was not afraid of any consequences that might come her way because of their failure to kill Yeltsin, if, in fact, he remained alive. She smiled at the thought of killing Yeltsin at some point in the future if that were the case. Irina fed on the adrenalin that came surging through her body. She lived to kill and the rush empowered her. In Irina's mind, the assignment may have failed, but there would be others beyond killing Yeltsin. At that moment, Irina pushed through and twisted around brush and trees, as alive as ever, in order to protect herself and insure her future.

§

The explosion rocked the entire house and sent the garage door flying off its rails. Smoke and dust blended to make seeing and breathing nearly impossible. Denis ended up halfway under Old Blue, the others were huddled together, coughing and rubbing their eyes, under Jack's workbench. Boris called out for Denis who had been returning fire. His blind search for his friend and bodyguard ended when he tripped over Denis's feet. "Comrade. Denis. Can you hear me?" Boris shook the man's boots then heard a groan and began to pull on the legs that protruded out from under the old truck. Jack made his way over to help as Denis finally appeared, bloody and dirty from being under the truck. The two men helped him to his feet as Dash jumped up on a set of tires then on to the workbench and out the broken garage window. Ellen called after him, but Dash disappeared down the street barking and dragging his leash.

Off in the distance, the whoop, whoop sound of helicopter blades increased as a giant spot light lit up the entire Sterling view Drive cul-de-sac. Neighbors came out of their homes and from behind bushes with disbelieving looks that reflected the carnage that had just taken place. Shouts asking for Jack and Ellen came from several people, including Ed. The neighborhood archer came running through the smoke, tripping over pieces of Jack and Ellen's house that lay in the driveway, out into the street, and spilling over into several neighboring yards.

The rancher-style home now had a giant hole where the larger of two garage doors had been, providing enough room for the four people inside to emerge. Janice came running down the street in time to see her husband appear like an apparition from the darkness. Ed had a bandana wrapped around his head. He resembled some Marvel super hero warrior looking for his plunder. "Eddie, are you all right, dear?" Janice shouted as she ran into his waiting arms. Her husband was wounded, that was all she could think about. Ed appeared to be stunned. "Where's, where's Jack and..." Ed stopped and leaned forward on Janice as an ambulance pulled up.

Bernard Jackson appeared on scene in time to flash his badge, looking for President Yeltsin. His men formed a perimeter around the area, rifles and handguns drawn. Yeltsin and Denis could be seen leaning against an old truck inside the partially destroyed garage. "Mr. President, are you alright, sir?" Yeltsin looked over at Jackson and asked for assistance. "Denis is hurt, he needs doctor."

A second ambulance crew were being escorted to the area

just in time to provide additional aid. The EMT's put Denis on a stretcher as Jackson ran up. He asked the crew to wait while they made an assessment on the patient's condition. Jackson had a schedule that allowed for very little wiggle room. A quick examination showed that Denis suffered a probable concussion, but, given the circumstances, would be able to travel once given medication.

The US Government had the return of Boris Yeltsin on a schedule, but there was the matter of the missing assassin. "Are you telling me that the man lying dead in this driveway is one of the assassins?" Jackson's sergeant looked at his commanding officer for a few seconds longer than normal, quickly adjusted, and confirmed the identification of Albert Trejenko, one of the world's most infamous assassins. Agent Jackson's schedule would have to be delayed, that he would handle. *Well planned actions had to have options.* They had to find a second person, according to the sergeant, identified as a woman. Trejenko was known to work alone. Whoever was behind this assault on Yeltsin, and this community, was dead serious about killing him. The protection of the Russian President just became more critical.

§

Chaos reigned all around Jack and Ellen Templeman's Eagle Ridge neighborhood. Debris flew up and swirled as the helicopter made low passes that ranged from the park down the hill to the quarry.

Boris and Denis were led to an awaiting Suburban, as police and fire vehicles began to arrive. One of the ambulance crew rolled a tarp over and around the dead man lying in Jack's driveway. Two military soldiers were posted to guard the corpse awaiting a military van.

Ellen talked to the neighbors while Jack discussed the possibility of chasing after the other assassin with Ed. Jack told the agents to listen for Dash, who Jack figured, was chasing the suspect. The little dog had run away toward the quarry, his bark could be heard off in the distance. "Shh. Listen." The personnel gathered near him waited a second and sure enough, they heard Dash's high-pitched barking echoing off the walls of the quarry. "Ed, are you up for a little more excitement?" Janice looked at her husband as if he were a superhero as Ed nodded his head. Off they went, heading down a short cut to the quarry.

Janice agreed to stay and watch over the Templeman's house, along with two other neighbor ladies. As they passed by the Suburban carrying Boris, the Russian spun and yelled to the line of men being led by Ed and Jack. "Wait, I need to see this man," Boris referred to Ed, who looked surprised to be called out. "Ed, my new friend. We worried for you. What happened?" Ed explained that he did take a shot to his arm, but it just grazed him. After he was hit, he laid still, hoping the shooter wouldn't come looking for him. He knew he wouldn't be happy with an arrow lodged in him. Ed stopped as Yeltsin gave him a big hug — gingerly, due to Ed's injured arm. Ed then introduced his wife, who'd been standing at his side listening.

"THE Boris...Yeltsin?" "Yes, madam. I'm hoping your Ed is feeling better soon. He is brave man, this Ed of yours. Pleasure to meet you." Janice's knees went weak as she shook the man's hand.

Before leaving with their escort, Boris requested that he see Jack. Bernard Jackson hesitated then nodded his head.

He understood the request and asked Jack to make it quick. Jack told Ed and the men to take off, he'd catch up. Jack smiled at Boris as they shook hands, each touching the other's shoulder. "Mr. President, I'm so glad you're not hurt." Boris smiled back as he put his hands together in a prayer position, pointing at Jack.

"Jack, my good American friend. It's time for me to leave. Please say goodbye to your lovely wife for me. And where is Dash?" Jack nodded and smiled. "Dash is the one barking out there somewhere." Jack pointed in the direction of the quarry. "Who is that?" Boris pointed in the direction of the man lying in the driveway, covered with a tarp and now guarded by police. "He's one of them, Boris." Denis offered, "I think Jack's dog is on the other one's trail."

The comment shocked Boris who'd been given just five minutes to say his goodbyes. "Jack, my hope is that you do well in life and especially on whatever stage you do your standup comedy. Remember, you belong there because you are funny." Boris pointed his finger in Jack's chest and then gave him another big hug. "I'm off now. May we meet again sometime."

Jack and Boris went their separate ways after that. Denis shook Jack's hand, nodding to him as if to say, good job.

§

Irina made her way through the heavily wooded area, ducking and weaving between branches that came out of the darkness like knives being tossed in her direction. The resulting wounds were more a nuisance than painful. She had to stay ahead of that little barking hound trailing her. She wanted to stop and shoot it, but running seemed the most prudent choice as she descended down a steep embankment. Irina went from running to sliding on her bum, holding onto bushes, branches and past a few boulders, until she came to a complete stop with her boots sticking straight out into the air up to her knees. She sat there feeling like she'd just been on one of her favorite amusement rides in Stockholm. Looking down about forty feet into a dimly lit open pit, she needed to make a decision and fast. Irina could see the street they had driven up and a few cars parked in driveways further down illuminated by street lights. All she had to do was get down there to complete her escape. "Well done, Comrade Trejenko." The truck was nearly invisible, he'd hidden it perfectly, facing out toward the street behind a bush-lined berm.

Irina began her descent down the slope as Dash ran up, barking and growling a few feet behind her. The dog's appearance threw the assassin off slightly, causing her to nearly lose her balance. She smiled at Dash, calling him a good dog, knowing he couldn't possibly follow. He looked bigger from her perspective. If he came any closer, she would cut his throat and throw him over the edge she now faced. Irina turned to look at the mutt as she made her way about half way down the steep slope, when suddenly she heard voices above and stopped. She checked her backpack, grabbed her handgun and a grenade. Irina didn't hesitate. She pulled the pin on the grenade and tossed it at the men, causing them to scramble. The dog retreated with two of the men as dirt, brush and rocks exploded in all directions. Irina covered herself and prepared to shoot whoever appeared above her, while still managing to keep her foothold on a protruding root from the tree above. The explosion bought her enough time to continue her escape as the men scrambled to recover.

A military helicopter flew low overhead with two spotlights roaming the landscape. The lights danced up and down the hillside. Irina took aim. One of the spotlights nearly blinded her as she took two perfectly aimed shots to provide cover for her next move. Both lights shattered on impact and the slope went dark again. The engine noise and wind coming from the chopper attempting to recover, threw her off her stride, as she shoved the gun into her pack and continued her descent. Sliding down an unknown hillside can be dangerous, especially at night. But considering the alternative, she had no choice. She was in luck, further down, the slope turned from rocks and tree roots to sand. Irina, to her surprise, managed to hit the base of the hill, running toward the truck.

The chopper pilot and the team of soldiers lost sight of the suspect, allowing Irina to enter the truck, start it and, with headlights off, exit the quarry going the opposite direction and down Lincoln Drive. The escape was on. She knew how to drive. Her last assignment included evasive maneuvers in a Lamborghini Gallardo with three times the horsepower of the Ford truck she now drove. Still, Irina adjusted well to the conditions that currently flew past her windshield. Driving without headlights could only last for a few more minutes, but so far, it was working. No helicopter spotlights from above and no sirens. When she hit the highway that ran parallel to Eagle Ridge, she headed north with headlights on and at four miles an hour over the posted limit. She would now become one of the crowd of cars and trucks that safely drove Highway 195.

§

The three Suburban caravan, with Boris Yeltsin and his bodyguard in the middle vehicle, approached the entrance to Fairchild Air Force Base. It was now or never for Bernard Jackson. His part in the plan to kill the man he'd been guarding would finally come to fruition. He'd had several opportunities over the last week to make the kill, but deferred to better judgment, which meant final authorization from the Vladimir Putin. Jackson had been a loyal American soldier for most of his career, that is, until he was approached while vacationing in Europe two years earlier. The offer was too good to refuse, besides, racial tensions had existed for far too long in the military, which also made his decision a lot easier.

Jackson had the sergeant pass the mic to him when they were approaching the turn lane into the Base. "Alpha and Beta make the turn onto the Base as planned, Delta will continue along the highway and enter the Base from the West. On my mark. Turn, now."

The sergeant looked up at his boss as the mic was returned. "Sir, why the change?" he whispered, hoping the others wouldn't notice. In a loud voice, Jackson turned and announced to the driver, his sergeant, Yeltsin, and the President's ailing bodyguard that the maneuver had been ordered at the last minute by Langley in order to throw off any threat following the caravan. "Turn here." The driver turned the Suburban onto a graveled service road that bordered the Base.

§

Eastbound traffic thinned out as Irina watched emergency vehicles racing west, lights and sirens blaring. The action made her nervous, as a result, she increased her speed. Driving at a higher rate of speed, Irina didn't notice the unmarked Washington State Patrol SUV parked along Highway 195. As she entered traffic, her truck caused a bus loaded with college students to hit the brakes, nearly resulting in an accident. The trooper monitoring traffic reacted immediately. The minute she passed him, he radioed his office that he was in pursuit, at a safe distance, and needed backup. He gave a description and license number of the negligent driver's truck. The description matched one that had just been given to authorities by a neighbor in Eagle Ridge, who had watched as a truck drove slowly out of the quarry and under the streetlight adjacent to her residence – without headlights.

After some careful driving and a break in traffic, the officer pulled up behind the truck and turned on his emergency lights. This was standard procedure on the less traveled highway. The hope was to stop the truck before it merged onto the more heavily traveled Interstate 90 about a half a mile ahead. The minute the emergency lights went on, the truck took off, causing the trooper to continue the pursuit from a safe distance and radio for more assistance.

§

"First it was the damn dog, now the authorities," she whispered to herself. The second she noticed the lights Irina knew what to do. She had studied the map they'd been given to find the target location. At Albert's suggestion, she had outlined two escape routes, both leading to the Canadian border north of their location. One of the routes went straight north from Spokane, the other went further east into Idaho before turning north. She decided to take the Idaho route, hoping that would buy her time and give her a better chance of escape.

The truck had just enough gas to reach the border if she stayed on the Interstate. She accelerated through traffic. As she did, she noticed that the trooper behind her had company. More lights behind her and now a beam of light from above illuminated the truck. She had to think faster. Traffic moved out of the way as she approached the Idaho state line at ninety miles an hour.

She had to get to Idaho. Up ahead the horizon lit up with warning lights as if it were on fire. The Interstate was suddenly barren, no vehicles. *ROADBLOCK. "Rohbo!"*

Irina headed for the nearest exit. That time of night made it difficult to stay on the exit at the speed she maintained. Irina tapped the brakes as she took the unexpected turn forty miles an hour faster than suggested. The truck did its best to remain on the roadway, but loose gravel on the shoulder made driving more difficult as she over-corrected and ended up weaving her way back under the freeway, changing lanes several times before coming to a stop on the roadside at the edge of a riverbank.

Irina exited the truck with her backpack on one shoulder and a long-range rifle on the other. As she ran for cover, Irina suddenly realized she hadn't eaten for nearly twelve hours. The hungry and thirsty assassin sat back and looked up at the stars in the sky wondering when she would see her homeland again. She longed to see the sky from her country rather than this foreign land that seemed to have her literally stuck in mud alongside a fast-running river. She could hear voices and dogs barking, *dogs again?*

Her training kicked in. She could last for a day or two on the two protein bars in her pack and bottled water. Sirens and shouting snapped her out of her momentary lapse. She would hide along the riverbank and hope to steal a car or truck later in the evening.

§

"Stop the car." The order sounded beyond official to the two officers accompanying Bernard Jackson. The moment the car stopped, Jackson shot and killed the driver and aimed his gun at the sergeant. They were in the middle of nowhere as far as Yeltsin was concerned. He'd made arrangements to have Dimitri ride in the Beta Suburban. The poor man will be so disappointed when Yeltsin goes missing for the last time. Jackson ordered his sergeant to hand over his gun and escort the two Russians out of the vehicle. "Hurry, move!" The sergeant complied and proceeded to help Boris and Denis out and onto the roadway. Denis was slow in reacting to the order and was shoved, by Jackson, to the ground as Yeltsin turned to face his adversary. "You will not treat us this way!" Yeltsin screamed at Jackson.

Jackson smiled at Yeltsin, raising his gun with both hands as he slowly walked toward the Russian leader. "You won't have to worry about how you are treated, Mr. President, at least not for much longer. I will personally see to it that you and your friend will never be found. You, sir, will be lost forever and forgotten."

Jackson ordered Yeltsin to his knees, next to Denis who began to sit up. In the excitement, Jackson had almost forgotten about his sergeant, who looked as though he stood ready to take another order. Jackson would eliminate him too, but not until after the Russian leader and his bodyguard were buried nearby.

"Sergeant, stand over by our visitors. Jackson tossed him a long-handled shovel he'd stored in the back of the SUV. With the barrel of a gun swinging between Yeltsin and him, the sergeant did as he was told. A slight breeze began to blow through the pine trees, slightly lowering the temperature. The sergeant fought off a chill in the air as he watched Jackson's every move. He knew there would be no reason for him to live much longer other than to dig graves. As Jackson walked to the backside of Yeltsin, the Russian leader followed his movement. Yeltsin raised his left hand and pointed a finger in Jackson's face. "You will be found out, Mr. Jackson, and shot for what you plan to do to us. You will not…"

"Stop talking." Jackson held the gun to Yeltsin's ear as he spoke, then brought it down, hard, on the back of the president's head. Yeltsin cried out in pain as Denis lunged at Jackson. He managed to shove Jackson hard enough that he lost his balance and rolled to one side. The CIA officer turned and quickly recovered. He aimed his gun at Yeltsin's bodyguard. "Rot in hell, Mr. President and take this animal with you." Jackson had barely finished his statement when the blade of the shovel hit him in his right shoulder, sending his gun flying and Jackson to the ground. Denis scrambled for the gun in competition with Jackson. Just as Jackson grabbed the handle of the gun, the shovel came around a second time, impacting the top of Jackson's head, knocking him out. Denis held the gun on Jackson as the sergeant ran to the Suburban and radioed for help. The sergeant returned a few minutes later. Boris watched as the sergeant used zip ties to secure Jackson's hands behind his back. "Are you hurt, sir?" Denis looked as if he was the one in pain. Boris assured him that he could walk, even though blood could be seen streaming down the side of his face. He then turned to look at the young sergeant.

"You have no idea what you've just done, sergeant." The young man stood looking down at his commanding officer lying face down in the roadside dirt. Denis handed over the gun and the sergeant pointed it at Jackson on the ground, who laid there moaning in pain. The sergeant knelt down and added a pair of steel handcuffs to the zip ties around Jackson's wrists, then stood up and asked Yeltsin and his bodyguard if they were okay. They both nodded and thanked the young man. "You are very brave, and also very skilled at placing handcuffs, sergeant." The two other Suburbans came racing up, each from different directions, skidding to a stop. Dimitri jumped out and took control of the situation from the sergeant as they loaded Jackson into one of the vehicles. On the way to the hangar where Yeltsin's flight back waited, Dimitri questioned the sergeant as to what had happened.

The sergeant shared with him that he became suspicious that something was wrong when Jackson somehow knew more than one assassin was involved. "He asked me to ID the man in the Templeman's driveway, but also knew the man's first name before I said it."

Chapter 10

SPOKANE VALLEY – SPOKANE RIVERBANK


The far-off barking angered Irina as she made her way along the gravel-strewn river bank. She had to stop and try to think between barking and shouts from the dog handlers. Part of her Red Sparrow training involved being blindfolded and left in the wilderness to be tracked down by dogs acting alone. The participants forage for themselves and were given two days to escape the drop zone and find camp before the dogs found them. Two of the ten participants were tracked down attempting to escape and were allowed to be mutilated by the dogs as punishment and a teaching moment. One of the victims, a good friend, tall, beautiful and funny, ended up being too slow to compete, mostly because of an ankle sprain, and gave up. That would not happen to Irina – she would fight.

In that exercise, the only weapon she had was her knife. The experience left an indelible mark on her soul and a long scar on her left thigh. Irina would rather take a blow to the head than be bitten by a large dog as she had been that day when she ran into camp, narrowly surviving the harrowing test. Seven of her fellow Sparrows who participated in the wilderness exercise graduated with her that year. She often wondered where in the world they were and what might have happened to them.

Irina shook her head to clear the cobwebs and gain more focus as she moved out into the water in order to throw the dogs off her scent. She made her way north and east in the water, three feet from the shore. The barking seemed to grow louder. Irina could tell that more dogs had been added to the tracking. That thought made her pick up the pace as she maneuvered her way, parallel to the shore, through junk and boulders, to a point under a concrete bridge.

Traffic moved at a fast pace above as she climbed up onto the bridge piling with a small ledge big enough for her to sit on. Irina sat there slapping her legs that had begun to go numb, hoping the dogs would lose her scent from the time she entered the water. She had driven about a mile into Idaho and the authorities were right on her tail. "That's not very hospitable," Irina thought as she scanned the area for anything that would float. Alongside a second bridge piling she spotted a log that had wedged itself between the piling and a boulder. The log slowly banged against the concrete, creating a dull, repetitious, thud. It took a few minutes, but she managed to free the timber and hook her back pack to it. Her immediate thought involved floating to the other side of the river where she could steal a car and make a run for it to the northern border. The plan seemed feasible enough, but she had to go, time was of the essence. The thought also reminded her to pee as she paddled.

Irina felt more relaxed as she reached for a broken branch on the topside of the log, large enough for her to hang onto. The water was refreshing at first, but soon she became cold and began to shiver. "Come on, legs, push, kick, th…that's it. She looked up at the headlights passing overhead. Out of the corner of her eye she saw flashlights combing the riverbank. Irina kicked silently with the log pulling her along as if designed to do so. Once the log entered the current, Irina nearly lost her handhold. She reset herself and hung on, trying to somehow steer the log to the other side, which turned out to be quite a challenge. After a few attempts at steering, she succeeded in finding an eddy where she let go, grabbed the pack and exited the river. She attempted to move quickly, but found trying to move her legs became a challenge. Thanks to high grass along the river, she could not be seen from the opposite side. Irina slapped at her legs to get the circulation flowing again. She walked slowly at first, and picked up speed as she continued for a few more minutes before reaching a service road. A short time later, after running in a low slinking motion, she located a farm.

Irina had managed to walk fast, undetected, a couple of miles from the freeway where the abandoned rental truck sat empty like an unwilling accomplice.

A white sign with green lettering greeted her as she cautiously slid between wooden rails of fence. The sign read: Welcome to the Hostenberry Farm. Irina could see people in what looked like a kitchen area of the house. She decided to stop sneaking and, Instead, walked straight up to the door and rang the bell. The older gentleman and his wife, who welcomed her into their farmhouse, invited Irina to rest. "You look tired, dear, let me take your clothes and dry them for you." Irina couldn't tell if the sweet-acting older lady had enough sincerity in her voice or not. Irina was too tired to tell. *I need to stay alert.* She declined, of course, and continued to stand as she prepared to eliminate the two in order to make off with their truck and some provisions, she was famished. Irina slid her backpack to the floor, making a clunking sound. Irina looked at the couple, then turned to unzip the pocket where she stored the gun. The man reacted by turning toward a closet nearby. Just as Irina reached inside for her gun, the lady threw a pan of boiling water at Irina, causing the assassin to scream as the man pulled his own gun on Irina from their pantry. She could tell he knew how to handle firearms. Irina was in pain froze as a few seconds ticked by on the kitchen clock. The lady had Irina's backpack and motioned for her to sit back in the chair. "Sit or be shot, your choice." The man's voice reinforced his abilities. The man's wife immediately tied Irina to a kitchen chair while the man called 9-1-1. Come to find out, the farmer also spent time as a volunteer with the local Sheriff's office. He and his wife heard about the freeway incident on their police scanner, which the man turned back on after making the call.

The local authorities later turned Irina over, within the hour, to Federal officers who were more than thankful to catch up with the notorious lady with burn marks on one side of her face. Eventually, Irina Dustakova ended up being held in a secret government location somewhere in the Midwest.

# Chapter 11

## EAGLE RIDGE

*One month later*

Monday mornings in Eagle Ridge can be hectic, especially around seven-thirty, with cars driving down the hill delivering kids to school and parents to work. Jack and Ellen embrace before leaving for work. Their home had been repaired, with final exterior paint yet to be applied.

It seemed as though every morning since the Boris Yeltsin incident, before leaving each other, they held their embrace just a little longer. "We have to be two of the luckiest people in this crazy world." Jack nodded at Ellen's sentiment and pulled her close as he added his own. "I'm so thankful you weren't hurt in all of the excitement." The two hugged again, and as they did, a low growl came from the floor below. Dash stationed himself in front of the muted television as a local newscast flashed a recent photograph of Irina Dustakova. Ellen laughed as Jack went over and turned off the television. Reaching down, he petted their furry little fighter. "Yes,

Dash, she was a bad person, but you are a very good dog." Dash wagged his tail and flew out the dog door and into his sanctuary, the backyard. Jack waited for Ed to pick him up for work, as it was Ed's turn to drive. Ellen was already on her way to the hospital and her shift caring for infants in the NICU. She had been away for a short time, which happened to be entirely too long.

Their time with Boris Yeltsin had been a surreal and frightening experience, which had been fully captured in the media locally and all over the world. As a result, Yeltsin's terrorizing bon voyage had brought them an unexpected amount of national prominence. Jack and Ellen accepted calls from a variety of reporters, writers and television producers looking for the "inside scoop" on what it had been like to hang with the notorious leader of Russia. One national broadcaster asked Jack if the rumor happened to be true that he and Boris Yeltsin had spent time playing chess together? "Yes, we played several times and I learned a lot from the man," Jack offered. Before the woman could ask a second question, Jack paused and added; "He's a clever player, a very good strategic thinker." Jack's comment made the interviewer laugh, which caught Jack by surprise. In defense of the Boris he'd come to like in such a short period of time, Jack had to interrupt the next question.

"Russia is fortunate to have a leader brave enough to guide them in a new direction." His comment stopped the interviewer dead in her tracks. The interview happened to be live, or Jack's comment, most likely, would have been edited out. Instead, the media interviewer went silent, smiled, and handed the mic to her cameraman, which officially ended the interview. "Ah...well, thank you mister Templeman. We're glad you and your wife are safe, as well as the rest of your neighbors who were involved in coming to President Yeltsin's aid." Most of the interviews lasted for several minutes, live on-air. One interviewer attempted to find out if Jack had learned of secret information that Yeltsin may have shared. Jack just smiled and simply uttered "No." In reality, though, Jack knew that Yeltsin had decided to change the way he approached his Presidential problems, because the man himself told him so. He said that if he remained President upon his return, his time in America would be considered a success.

The interviews stopped abruptly once Boris Yeltsin returned and order was restored in Russia. The last interview/story centered around the possibility of a Boris and Jack reunion at some point. When asked by an *Orlando Herald* reporter what Jack thought of the idea, Jack was quoted as saying, "I would welcome a reunion with President Yeltsin, but only if we could meet in a Russian comedy club. I would like to catch up with Mr. Yeltsin and visit his country, but I'd have to learn the language if he wanted me to tell a few jokes." A short time later, Jack received an email from his Russian friend. In all caps it read: "You and Ellen are welcome to visit once we repair roads and relationships. That may take a week or a century. Just joking."

Life in Eagle Ridge and at work seemed to be getting somewhat back to normal.

On his way to work, this time with Ed in the passenger seat, Jack stopped off at Chi Chi's Better Brew. The two-sided latte stand stood in the corner of the local grocery store parking lot, down the hill from the quarry. The area also included a bank, hair salon, and two restaurants. Chi-Chi and Ellen went to nursing school together and worked at the same hospital until Chi-Chi developed a passion for roasting coffee. Jack saw Chi-Chi serving customers in the car ahead as he drove up. It had been too long since his last visit. Between the media attention and healing from their wounds, Jack and Ed had been laying low. Jack scrambled for the punch card in the center console as they watched Chi-Chi do her thing at the drive-up window. She acted like delivering well-brewed coffee orders required a certain skill with an entertaining twist. To Chi-Chi, the world needed to know her and her coffee blends in that order. Big hoop earrings, spray tan, yellow dress, and a big smile accompanied by an infectious laugh, added to the satisfaction of every customer, including Jack.

"Hey, Jack. How's Boris Yeltsin's best buddy? And your sidekick, The Archer." It wasn't as if Jack hadn't expected the comment, but it did stop him for just a second. "Hello, Jack, are you there, Jack? Earth to Jack Templeman!" Ed couldn't stop laughing.

"Chi, Chi I'm living the dream. How about a…"

"Stop, I got it ready already, saw you in line. I have Eddie's too, a triple 20 oz. Mayan Mocha, for our local heroes. Am I right, boys?"

When Jack reached for his wallet to pay, Chi-Chi raised a hand and let him know that drinks were on the house for the men, wounded in action, who brought international attention to the Eagle Ridge area. Not only that but, two assassins, the Feds, cops, fire trucks, a chopper, guns blazing and bombs that really made a lot of noise. She pointed at him as he drove off. "You are the man, Jack-o. Give Ellen a hug. Bye Eddie."

§

Jimmy stood in Jack's parking spot at City Hall as he and Ed pulled up. They exited the car with drinks in hand, but before they could say a word, Jimmy started talking. "Jack, I just heard that the mayor is planning some kind of press conference this morning, you and Ed are going to be in the spotlight. "What?" Jack had taken some additional time off, but was ready to get back to work and forget being the center of attention.

"I don't need this, Ed." Jack asserted after taking a drink of his mocha.

"I'm pretty sure both of you are expected to be in the City Council Chambers at ten. The weekly Monday morning meeting was canceled and both of you are the reason." Jimmy looked sheepish at having to share, what he thought was good news. He didn't know what to expect from Jack, but hoped that both of the men he looked up to would join in the celebration – *they deserved it.*

Jack put his arm on Jimmy's shoulder as the three walked across the parking lot, heading for their office. Jimmy always enjoyed listening to Ed and Jack's conversations. He learned so much about City Hall, politics, and more recently, comedy. Jimmy had been bored at work for nearly a month without his two mentors.

The security guard shook each one of their hands as the three made their way through the search area. When they reached the elevator, Jimmy couldn't help but notice employees smiling and pointing at the threesome. "I think you guys are famous." Jack hurried them into an empty elevator as he let Jimmy's statement float while Ed looked straight ahead. "Well, you *are.* I mean, the mayor even wants to recognize your bravery. Jimmy's last comment caused Jack to push the STOP button. Jimmy slowly moved to the back, not knowing what was about to happen. "Jimmy, nice shirt by the way, also, you need to know, Mayor Walters is a whack job most of the time. Whatever he's up to, it will be to *his* benefit, not ours." Jack just stood there for a second, Ed looking at Jack, Jack looking straight at Jimmy, who thanked Jack for the shirt comment, and was relieved when the doors finally opened. The three proceeded to their respective desks and got right to work.

Ed sported a large bandage that covered most of the left side of his partially shaved head, a second wound that he received while being chased. Even though it wasn't an easy time for him, he tried to answer every question asked of him. Whenever a reporter asked how Ed felt about wounding and eventually taking the life of the male assassin, he explained that his intention was to disable the assassin and keep him from hurting his friends. The first shot wounded the male assassin with a bolt, before the assassin doubled back to locate the archer. "It had to be a lucky shot on my part, because there wasn't much light. I could see everything play out from my vantage point, it was a very nervous time for me, until he aimed his gun at Jack. I set my sight on the reflection of the gun and let the bolt go." Jack told Ed he had the look of a veteran warrior, after the wounded assassin caught up with Ed and shot him, twice. "The doctor said I was fortunate. The assassin's first bullet grazed the scalp and didn't affect the skull. I didn't feel that shot as much as the one in my shoulder." There was a pause, then Ed added: "I didn't mean to kill the guy, Jack, but he was ready to launch that grenade." Jack reassured Ed that he did the right thing. "Hey, we helped save the President of Russia and his bodyguard. Not many people can put that on their resumes." Speaking of Boris, Ed, what did you think of his press conference last night?"

The nightly news featured Boris Yeltsin with his version of his disappearance and eventual rescue. Finally, the fullstory began to unfold in the media. The U.S. Government and the Russian authorities did their best to keep the Eagle Ridge incident, and the American federal protection for Boris, from the public. But the truth leaked out when Boris acknowledged his American assistance.

Ed touched the bandage on his head as he replied, "I thought Boris did a brilliant job."

Jack looked as if in a trance as he listened to Ed's comment while staring out his office window. He acted like he'd never seen the Spokane River from his second-floor viewpoint before. "Yes, he's a politician and had to be careful about what he said."

"That's not what I'm talking about, Jack." Ed sounded adamant. Jack snapped out of his trance and apologized for making Boris sound insincere. He told Ed he knew what he meant. "I agree, Boris is a very brave man – and a strong leader. He's also our friend." Both men nodded to one another and returned to work.

§

Boris Yeltsin appeared back in Moscow after hiding out in the Russian state of Tbilisi for the last two weeks, with his family. Boris rode to the event in a military tank, sharing the turret with a soldier waving the Russian flag. The media caught the end of the ride, which included several more tanks and military vehicles. As the tank carrying the Russian leader slowed, Boris climbed up further prepared to address the thousands of people forming around him. An enormous crowd gathered outside the Russian parliament building. Boris waved to the crowd as they chanted his name in unison.

An officer stepped forward and handed him a microphone. Once the crowd settled down, he began his speech.

"This is a new day for Russia. It is time for all to come together, unified, one nation of industrious people willing to celebrate the past as we open our minds to a new society in the future. I, Boris Yeltsin, ask: Are you ready and willing to change? We have spent so much time and energy trying to indoctrinate – why not collaborate? When I travel around Russia from now on, I'd like to see more smiles and hear the laughter that's been hiding deep inside us all for too long. Laughter versus insults and negative feelings will help to create a much healthier Russia. A very wise man recently told me that he would rather hear people laugh, than inherit wealth. According to my new friend, you can't put a price on happiness."

Yes, Boris Yeltsin actually referred to Jack. Ed knew it, Jack knew it, and most importantly Boris felt it necessary to recognize his new friend for suggesting *Happiness* be implemented into his political speeches. Before Boris went any further, he told two jokes that he and Denis came up with during their return. The reaction from a stunned crowd, eventually, became positively overwhelming with encouraging shouts and applause.

News spread that something strange had happened to President Yeltsin during his hiatus. The questions then became: Who is Boris Yeltsin now? And what would that mean for the future of Russia?

§

Ellen found an inside parking space, her goal every time she went to work at the Medical Center near downtown on the South Hill. It helped to know after her twelve-hour shift that she wouldn't have to deal with any bad weather situations. After parking her car on the fourth level of the parking garage, she headed for the third lower level and the hospital's cafeteria. She needed coffee, a 16oz. breve latte with sugar free caramel, before meeting her colleagues in the NICU. As she rounded the corner from the elevator that led into the cafeteria, she noticed her supervisor sitting at one of the first tables.

"I was hoping to catch you, Ellen." Sharon Landers, an RN working in administration, had twenty years of experience with babies in the Neonatal Intensive Care Unit. Sharon helped to create the department she now managed and became, in every way, Ellen's role model.

"Sharon, what a surprise." "I'm buying, Ellen, but you have to know that I'm, we, are all curious about what happened in Eagle Ridge, and how you and Jack are doing."

Ellen would miss the first thirty minutes of her shift, talking with her boss, answering questions that seemed even more unbelievable as she relived the Russian experience during their impromptu Q & A. One of the tougher questions to answer was what she thought of Boris Yeltsin. "He and Jack really hit it off. Boris impressed me as a very sensitive individual, someone who really cares about people. I hope he and his family are safe." Sharon had a look of satisfaction as she escorted Ellen to the ninth floor NICU. When Sharon left, Ellen took a deep breath, and for the first time that morning, it was her turn to ask a question as she entered a pod and looked over one of their newest arrivals – just hours old. "Well, well young lady, what do we have here? Poopy pants?

§

Ellen called Jack the minute she received confirmation from Janice about Jack's idea. Jack came up with what he referred to as a *brainstorm* late last night. He wanted the real hero of the assassination attempt on Boris, their dog Dash, to show up that morning at City Hall. The only way for that to happen was if someone would agree to stop by the house and transport him to City Hall in time for the mayor's gathering. Janice happily volunteered. Jack wanted it to be a surprise for everyone, including Ed.

"Janice is in the lobby with Dash," Ellen whispered into her phone as she entered the nurses' station after taking a call from Janice.

"Perfect timing. Ask her to come to the Council Chambers."

Jack and Ed entered the City Council Chambers to a rousing round of applause and a few whistles. Mayor Walters, with his big toothy campaign smile gleaming brightly, motioned the Planning Department duo to join him at the podium. A dozen or so of the 60 people gathered knew otherwise, as the mayor acted as if he were encouraging old friends to the stage. Both men stood at the door looking at each other and then back at their cheering audience. Jack whispered to Ed, "I guess it's too late to leave gracefully." Ed gave Jack a little push, but Jack hesitated and motioned for Ed to open the door behind them. The door opened to Janice standing with Dash on a leash, wagging his tail. Once the dog saw Jack he began to walk slowly into the Chambers. Ed couldn't believe it as Janice handed over the leash, which Ed passed on to Jack who greeted the furry hero. "Hey little man, this is your day too." All three started for the stage, Dash leading the way. Janice joined in the cheering as she stood inside the Chambers.

The mayor, surrounded by his team, including Fenton and Corrine, two people who would rather see Jack tarred and feathered instead of being heralded for bravery, led the cheers. The entire team had their fake smiles turned on as the mayor welcomed the "Brave and courageous duo, oh, and their dog." Someone called out "Dash."

When asked to say a few words, Jack responded right away with a big wave as he replaced the mayor at the podium. "Thank you all for taking the time out of your busy schedules, and you too Mr. Mayor." As Jack spoke, Dash decided to wander around by the podium, flirting with various employees with a smile and wag of his tail.

"What happened in Eagle Ridge that day will, no doubt, be remembered in history forever. Hard to believe, but it's true, we, America, saved the life of the President of Russia." Jack pointed to the crowd from one side to the other as he spoke. "The man standing next to me, Ed La Drew (pause for applause) is, without a doubt, one of the bravest people I know. He's also very good with a crossbow, so watch yourself around here." Jack's comment drew a round of laughter and more applause. Most people had seen Ed interviewed on national television, including "Good Morning America" a week earlier. Jack then turned his attention to Dash, who, by that time, stood closer to Jack. He bent down and picked up the little guy. "Some of you remember Dash, our dog. He's been to City Hall before." The comment caused the mayor to clear his throat and look at Ms. Bundle. "Dash is also a hero." The fury hero barked as Jack let him down. The dog had also been featured in a media story as the real reason one of the assassins was later captured. Jack finished and shook hands with people who came forward to pet Dash, which he enjoyed, as the festivities wound down.

The ceremony, if one chose to call it that, lasted longer than the mayor intended, partially because of Jack Templeman's unexpected guest. The mayor's attempt to be in the spotlight more than Jack, Ed and Dash, failed. When Fenton reached down to pet Dash, Ms. Bundle pulled him back, "He's one of them." But several people from the mayor's staff later got a lick or two from Dash.

Jack referred to the impromptu event celebrating the safe return of President Yeltsin and showcasing the City Hall heroes that participated in the effort as "One of City Hall's strangest moments." He made a mental note to work the occasion into one of his upcoming comedic routines.

Janice came forward and took Dash back home. She called Ellen at work to give her a report on what happened. She didn't have to say much, because the media had been invited and they both agreed that the news reporters would have a field day with the fact that Mayor Walters took a backseat to a dog.

Back in his office, Jack closed the door and sat in quiet solitude. His mind wouldn't stop thinking about the night Boris Yeltsin left Eagle Ridge. Jack had never come that close to dying and the more he thought about it, the more he knew he had to put it behind him and get on with life. Still, he couldn't overcome the feeling that there was something about meeting Boris Yeltsin that made him feel better about facing his future. *Courage*, plain and simple. That was it. The man never showed fear at any time. Jack promised himself to use the time he had with Boris wisely by incorporating that attribute in his life.

Back to reality. Jack went through his list of work projects, including the new development in Eagle Ridge. He carefully opened the tube of work plans and spread them out on his slanted work table and carefully pinned the edges down. Immediately, he found the location of the under-construction house they had used as refuge the night they ran from the two assassins chasing them. Jack put his hand over the area where Boris and Denis stayed on Pinehurst Drive and began to trace the escape route they took that night. When his hand reached the unfinished house where they stopped to catch their breath, the one Ed remained in, while the rest went on, there was a knock on his closed door. Jack jerked his hands away from the table in response. His heart was racing, then realized what had just happened as he looked at the door, as if it was going to tell him something. The door opened in slow motion. Jimmy's head appeared and then the rest of him as if he were being inflated from some hidden source. "Hey Jack, here's your mail." Jack sat up quickly with that *you surprised me* look on his face.

Jimmy handed Jack a large bundle of mail and two small packages. As he slowly backed out, Jimmy added. "Didn't mean to startle you, Jack, sorry." Jack held up a reassuring hand as he replied, "I'm fine, Jimmy. You just surprised me, that's all." He sat back down in his desk chair locked in a starring contest with his journeyman planner. "Jimmy?"

"Oh, sorry, glad you're back, Mr. Templeman. Ah, there's someone here to see you. Says... well, he has a badge." Jimmy's last comment brought Jack forward in his chair. Jimmy stood in the doorway waiting for Jack's response. Jack stood, thanked Jimmy and walked to a small waiting area where he greeted a young man in a Marine uniform.

"Mister Templeman, I'm Sergeant Roble."

"I recognize you, sergeant. But from where?" Jack hesitated and suggested they go to his office. Behind closed doors, Sergeant Hank Robel explained that he worked with the detail monitoring President Yeltsin's movements, during Yeltsin's stay in Eagle Ridge. And the sergeant accompanied President Yeltsin and his bodyguard to Thule airbase on the return trip. "The President made the request himself. I couldn't believe it." He didn't go into what had happened to his commanding officer, Bernard Jackson, who turned out to be a traitor working with the Russians. Instead, he chose to thank Jack for his quick action in protecting President Yeltsin. "The whole situation could have been catastrophic for the State Department if something had happened to him." Jack didn't know what to say. In his mind, if our State Department had done a better job of diplomacy, there wouldn't have been a need to help. But he held his tongue as the sergeant reached into his jacket pocket and handed Jack an envelope. "He wanted me to give this to you, personally."

Jack already had a stack of mail about six inches high sitting on his desk. After the Marine left, he made quick work of separating the "clutter" from the "necessary mail." Topping the new stack was a legal-size envelope with a U.S. Government seal on it. Picking up the envelope, he joked to himself on finding that it was hand addressed. "Who in the federal government would be contacting him?" Jack had plenty to catch up on, but this envelope intrigued him, because it was from his former neighbor. Sitting back down at his desk, he cleared a spot and opened the letter and began to read.

*Dear, Jack. I'm writing to you from somewhere over Greenland. There was no time for me to thank the one person*

*who I have come to know as my only real American friend.
We choose our friends, thank goodness, others are either related
or get in our way most times. But you, Jack, I consider to
be a special friend. What you did for me, and Denis, I will
always remember. Like our chess matches and the laughter-filled
conversations we had related to life, and how it is important
to find humor, even in times of sorrow. You have touched me
in such a positive way – I am more committed to leading my
people. I want you to know that. I also hope this letter will
reach you and encourage you to move forward with your comedy.
You are a funny man, Jack. What we went through together
that last night in your Eagle Ridge may not be funny, but you
are the one person I know who will find humor in the least
likely place. That takes talent, Jack. And talent should never
be wasted.*

*Be well and please say hello to your lovely Ellen and that
rascal Dash.*

*Your Friend,*
*Boris.*

Jack sat back in his chair and smiled as he finished the note from Boris. He carefully folded the page and replaced it in the envelope. "Boris thinks I'm funny," Jack whispered as if he finally convinced himself. Immediately, he began to laugh, thinking about his one in-a-million-chance opportunity to meet a foreign leader who now calls him a friend. He almost fell out of his chair as he kicked backward. Pulling himself back upward, his laughter changed to a more solemn feeling of concern for Boris and his family. They will always be targets. Boris will always be looking over his shoulder as he carries the enormous burden of leadership he'd chosen. And yet, he took the time to write a letter of encouragement.

Jack stood up and looked out his window thinking to himself. "Alright, Boris, I will find the humor – my friend."

§

Two weeks later, Jack stood backstage going over his notecards at Peabody's Laugh Emporium. Jerry Peabody gladly worked Jack into the lineup, especially after hearing and reading about his unbelievable experience with Boris Yeltsin in the newspaper and on TV. Jack Templeman already proved himself to be a good comic, locally. Now, with his recent exposure nationally, maybe it was time for him to become a bona fide comedian. What a great story, Jack, back on stage, an ordinary guy who'd become an international celebrity, because of all the media exposure. It surprised Jerry actually. After all the excitement that he'd been through, Jack found time to put a comedy set together. That amazed the comedy club owner.

"Our next comedian is a local who you may recognize unless you've been living underground for the last month or so. Yes, he considers Boris Yeltsin a close buddy, and I'm sure he'll have something to say about that. Here he is, for a return engagement, the one and only comedian to call City Hall his home away from home. Please give a warm Peabody's welcome to Mister Jack Templeman."

The spotlight that hit Jack as he walked on stage, wiped out the faces of half the audience. He expected that. What he didn't expect was how calm he felt. The applause grew louder as he neared the microphone in the middle of the stage with a bottle of water and a stool. He set the stool down, placed the bottle next to it and turned to face the audience. People yelled and whistled. "Thank you. What a great crowd. Are you guys sure you're in the right place?" Finally, the applause ended with Ellen's familiar, high-pitched, whistle. The silence that suddenly came over the place felt welcoming to him. The "City Hall Comedian" took a deep breath, smiled to an audience he could only feel at first, until his eyes became used to the glare.

Jack reached for the mic and removed it from the stand. "Thank you, good citizens of the Republic of Spokane. (laughs and hoots) Sorry, my newfound relationship with the Russian leader must have rubbed off. By the way, that last long whistle came from my wife Ellen, stand up sweetheart." (applause) Ellen is a NICU nurse at the Medical Center. (more applause) She uses that whistle at home to call our dog, Dash, when he wanders off. She also uses it at work. Oh, yeah, honestly. When feeding time is over for those little ones, she lets out a big whistle and the bottles come flying from all directions. Hey, it's what makes her special."

Jack was on a roll. He asked Ellen to remain standing and demonstrate, but she politely refused, blushing and covering her face. (More applause) Jack took a breath and a drink of water as the laughter subsided. He put one arm over the mic stand and in a low voice doing his best Russian accent uttered: "So, vile da whole vorld vas lookink for Comrade Yeltsin last mont, vee vere playink chess een Eagle Ridge…Gott, I hope my vife und I don't get into trouble over invitink heem here to Peabody's. You tink I'm kiddink." Jack pointed at some people at a front table as if calling them out. "I'll just let you imagine that Boris and his bodyguard did make the show" – and they laughed. "Ya. Boris tinks I'm funny. Imagine dat."

The set went as hoped and ended when Jack pulled two small flags out his pocket – one Russian and the other

American. His jokes were full of the most frightening details that actually happened the night of the Terrorist Invasion of Eagle Ridge. But the perspective he took made the situation look so ridiculous, it became funny. From running with Boris and his bodyguard, to the bolts being shot at international terrorists, the incident became a seriously funny happening that evening. Jerry Peabody stood off stage drinking coffee watching the crowd reactions. He loved seeing people just let themselves go the instant a comic hits them with an unexpected line or mannerism. Everything Jerry had hoped for Peabody's manifested itself in what he was witnessing at that moment. He promised himself to have a serious talk with Jack about his future in comedy. Soon.

Jack kicked it into high gear. Earlier in the week, He met with Fred and Amy Brewster in their home. The president of the Eagle Ridge HOA asked if he would find out how they were coping after their home invasion. Jack agreed. Besides, he and Ellen felt bad about what the Brewster's must have encountered. Jack sat across from Fred as Amy brought a tray of tea and cookies to the dining room table. As the older gentleman began, Jack noticed part of Fred's left eyebrow was missing, probably the result of duct tape being pulled from his face. Jack tried not to look at the spot, but he had to restrain himself. Jack focused and the more he heard the more he couldn't believe his ears. Jack never intended on putting the Brewster's experience in a future show, but there it was, on a platter. Fred explained, in detail, how he and his wife had been duct taped, Amy's incessant humming of Amazing Grace, and their mutual manner of escaping, rocking together. Jack could hardly write fast enough when he returned home.

Jack had the audience imagine the Brewster's experience,

without identifying them, and people hit the floor laughing. Their terrifying experience with international assassins only became funny because it was based on real-life trauma. You just couldn't make up the invasion of a home by international terrorists in the Pacific Northwest. And Jack's interpretation of it made it seem even more ridiculous. "Honestly, if it were up to me, I would have tried to get my wife to hum a medley of her favorite religious tunes. Maybe, "This Little Light of Mine" or "When the Saints Come Marching In"? But good for them, they did manage to escape… and stay married."

# Chapter 12

## MOSCOW, RUSSIA

### *September 1993*

Boris returned to Russia a changed man. Although he had a number of fiscal issues to confront, Boris prepared himself to meet them head on as soon as he hugged his wife and children. The President of Russia had an even larger target on his back, causing him to be even more selective when choosing his inner circle. People, like Denis, who believed in him.

Denis left for a few days to be with his family, but returned to the Kremlin, where Boris had settled – refreshed and ready. The Soviet Union had been dissolved and it was time to move forward with a new Russia.

The price of oil was in decline and the value of the ruble continued to fall. As the first President of modern-day Russia, he wanted to introduce new policies to the Russian people that would complement communistic ideals. He had failed at hard sells before, but Boris had a new way to approach his constituents and those who opposed him. Included in his notes that contained, new, more specific goals were humorous anecdotes. The format was risky, but it was a risk he had to take. *Lighten up, comrades!*

Since his decision to move from the White House, formerly the Russian House of Soviets, to the Kremlin, he'd been busy working with his close advisors to create an agenda that would begin to heal some of the more devastating issues Russia faced. One of his first orders was to have a national broadcast that would present his new plan. He wanted it to be from a stage outside the White House with Russian dignitaries, including military leaders. All were invited to attend with a one-line disclaimer: YOUR ATTENDANCE DEEPLY APPRECIATED – ABSENCE DULY NOTED. Part of Boris's agenda included his shifting view of the Communist Party of the Soviet Union, since the dissolution of the Union. He wanted to be known as the President who directed Russia into a more productive future by changing the old ways of Karl Marx and Vladimir Lenin. He couldn't worry about what the Party thought as he moved closer to including more capitalistic successes into Russia's everyday life. Why couldn't Russia be successful in providing full grocery store shelves and fast-food restaurants?

Boris sat back from his desk as he recounted his time in the United States. He laughed to himself when he thought of his pseudonym: Yuri Blachenko. In fact, his laughter evoked a response from his secretary, Luka, who came running. "Mr. President. Are you all right, sir?" Boris turned in his chair to face the man who'd been at his side for the last ten years. "Of course, Luka, why did you think something was wrong?" "You, you were… laughing, sir."

Luka's comment hit Boris hard. The man was right. Boris had found it easier to laugh since his return, that he credited to Jack, one hundred percent. "Luka, don't be fooled by laughter, enjoy it. Feel it. Be good with it. (pause) Try it." Luka stood up straight, the full length of revealed mostly perfect teeth, except in two places where he lost teeth during his recent interrogation. His hand brushed back his black hair as he stood at attention. "I am ready, sir."

"Ready for what?"

"Are you going to share what you were laughing about, sir, so I can do the same?" Luka's comment made Boris laugh again, only harder, which became infectious. Soon, the room filled with laughter, causing more interest from others located in nearby offices.

Communist Party factions continued to work vigorously, behind the scenes, to oust Yeltsin. They grew tired of the President's continual support for a more Western-style of thinking when it came to expanding Russia's economy. Business relationships with companies like; British Petroleum, John Deere and Boeing made more sense than entertaining; Gucci, McDonalds, Nike and Pepsi. And Yeltsin himself appeared to have changed. He had more confidence and smiled more. He even included a few jokes in his speeches, now and then, which surprised his audiences and infuriated opposition Party members. More attention needed to be paid to bolstering the military strength of the country, a priority that had reigned for centuries.

Colonel Alexander Rustkoy could not be trusted and was asked to step aside from his duties as Military Chief-of-Staff by Yeltsin. The Colonel didn't take the demotion well. Yeltsin tried to make the change appear as though the man was close to retiring and needed to slow down. Boris even worked the crowd invited to a press conference by offering a few jokes in order to lighten the mood. Rustkoy's replacement, Colonel Sergey Baskin, who had been jailed during Yeltsin's disappearance, shared the stage with Rustkoy, the man who had him incarcerated.

That replacement decision, as well as a continuing problem with inflation, combined to challenge the Yeltsin Administration for years. The people of Russia were divided between the old ways and the possibility of a new, more modern style of living. Older citizens, nearly sixty per cent of the population, were used to being told what to do and how to live. They were more reluctant to change than the younger adults who welcomed any opportunity to embrace western influences, especially if they included a Big Mac with fries and a Coke. As a result, a political tug-of-war between the opposing factions reared its ugly head. The opposition to Yeltsin's radical plan resulted in the loss of many good people on both sides before the final blows came to pass in the late '90's. Boris Yeltsin's time as President came to an end in 1999. A man Boris felt he once had on his side, Vladimir Putin, became the President of Russia, proclaiming to create a new future, based on what he had learned from his years of service under Boris Yeltsin. By the time Boris walked from the Kremlin for the last time, he knew the people of Russia were in for a more dictatorial reign of power. Putin could credit Yeltsin all he wanted, and for all appearances and intentions, the people were putting their trust in Vladimir Putin. Eventually, Putin showed that he was tied to the dictates that had been given him by the Communist Party.

§

The last half of the last decade of the twentieth century happened to be very good for Jack Templeman. The man formerly known as the "Guy from City Hall" became "Boris Yeltsin's Chess Partner," a rising star at Peabody's Comedy Club. The media coverage surrounding the disappearance of Boris Yeltsin and his eventual rescue put Jack's comedy career into overdrive. In fact, Jack, Ellen and Dash, each had more than their fifteen minutes of fame, but Jack's time naturally was extended, as he used his life-changing experience to feed his comedy. One of Jack's funniest routines came from his discovery of the "Mustached" neighbor. Jack would take the audience through his dog-walking tangle up with Dash to the time he entered Boris's (a.k.a. Yuri's) residence on Pinehurst Drive, expecting to enforce HOA landscaping codes. By the time Jack described attempting to pass by Boris's "No Neck" bodyguard, without wetting himself, and ended up playing chess with the federally protected, President of Russia, the audience was ready to pass out with laughter. "Did not see the chess board coming," Jack would say looking anxiously at his audience.

Within a few weeks, it became obvious to Jerry Peabody that Jack had the potential to become a big player on the comedy stage, not only in Spokane, but on the national circuit. After completing his second weekend of soldout shows, Jack met with Jerry for breakfast and serious discussion concerning Jack's future as a comedian. "Jack, there are people who tell jokes for a living and there are real comedians who make people laugh by telling stories. You, sir, have become the latter, which is good, because real comedians make more money for themselves and the people who present them, like me."

Jack sat back in his chair, took a sip of orange juice, and smiled at his gray-haired comedy guru. He already knew that his status as a member of Jerry's comedy club had been elevated. But unlike most of the amateur jokesters at Peabody's, Jack didn't perform for money. His goal was to make people laugh. It was the ultimate thrill to share a thought with a quiet, room full of people hanging on his every word, and making them burst into side-splitting laughter as the punchlines are delivered.

Jerry offered to connect Jack with an agent he knew in Los Angeles. After Jerry said that, Jack couldn't hear another word coming from the man sitting across from him. Jerry's mouth moved, but his words were on mute. Jack's imagination took over and for the next few moments he tried to wrap his head around entertaining in front of thousands in a stadium or even millions of fans on television.

"Jack? Jack, are you okay?" Jack nearly broke his neck as he suddenly came out of his trance. "Jerry. Sorry, I was off somewhere. I heard what you said about an agent, and I appreciate your willingness to make that connection. I'll have to discuss this with Ellen of course." Jerry understood and told Jack that he shouldn't wait too long. The media exposure would soon wear off and Jack needed to *strike while the iron was hot*. Jack left the meeting with his head spinning.

Weeks became months as Jack's short window of opportunity began to disappear like the wounds from that terrifying night. Even though Ellen was willing to go with whatever Jack wanted to do, they both decided that it was more important to be famously happy at home rather than taking a chance on becoming a celebrity.

Instead, Jack and Ellen decided on saying yes to a decision they'd been considering for years − starting a family − and eventually had two children, Tiffany, after Ellen's favorite aunt, and Mick, after Jack's favorite baseball player growing up: Mickey Mantle. Jack remained at City Hall, but Ellen decided to become a stay-at-home mom, having spent nearly fifteen years in the NICU.

With the advancement of digital communications, Jack was able to keep in touch with Boris after the man became the *former* President of Russia. Jack would share his comedy with the man who had become his biggest fan, even though Jack decided not to take his comedy any further than Spokane. "I'm sure people laugh just as hard in your Spokane as anywhere else, Jack," Boris would write in his emails. The two remained in contact even though Jack would read about Boris's problems health wise. When he asked him about it in an email,

Boris denied it and added: *I have lived, loved and laughed. What more can a man ask for?*

A personal email from Boris's wife confirmed his death. The men corresponded on a regular basis, so it was easy for her to find Jack's email address. The former President hadn't been feeling well and was hospitalized in April of 2007. Twelve days later, he died from cardiac arrest. Once Jack had a chance to rehearse it, he returned Mrs. Yeltsin's email asking if it was possible to attend Boris's funeral. She let Jack know that it will take three weeks to coordinate the funeral, they would be very welcome to come, and not to make hotel reservations. YOU AND YOUR WIFE ARE WELCOME TO STAY WITH ME. Ellen made arrangements for the children to stay with relatives. She also received permission to add Ed and Janice to their flight schedule, as all four were able to make their way to Moscow, Russia.

The four were met at Pushkin International Airport

by an old friend and close associate of Boris's. The stocky blond-haired man stood, waving his hands and smiling, in the international lobby. As the foursome passed through customs and began the long walk to the front entrance, Ellen was the first to notice the familiar face. "It's Denis, look, over there." What an unexpected, but welcomed, greeting for them. An emotional moment, full of hugs and a few tears, in the middle of a huge lobby, with people hurrying all around. Denis helped with luggage as they made their way to his van parked nearby. "You have made it in time for funeral, we are all happy to see you. Boris would be very pleased."

The funeral turned out to be the first religious ceremony in 113 years, for a former head of state, to be celebrated in a church. Very few people knew that President Yeltsin celebrated his faith on a regular basis. It was his desire to be buried in a casket by a Russian Orthodox priest. Boris's wife showed her appreciation for the Americans that came to share in Boris's celebration of life by giving them a framed picture and one of two presidential rings. "He always thought of you, Jack, as friend," she told him at the graveside, tears flowing. "We are so grateful that you made him feel welcomed in your community and that you made him smile." Jack just nodded knowing he couldn't say a word. The four visiting Americans left the next day for Saint Petersburg, Russia. Ed and Janice arranged a short cruise on the North Sea and then a flight home from Copenhagen.

The years that followed had Jack spending more time with his growing family and traveling, mostly camping, with Dash leading their four children through the Rocky Mountain foothills of the Pacific Northwest. Comedy became an occasional pastime for Jack. He was happy to be the local celebrity who had befriended Boris Yeltsin and beat him at chess. Every time he returned to the stage at Peabody's and looked out over the crowd, he did his best to be funny and make his family and Boris proud.

## The End

# Author's Notes

Boris Yeltsin earned the right to be mentioned in history as have many other revolutionary thinkers. He captivated me with his bold attempt to modernize an archaic communist system. There are people we look up to because we will emulate them somehow. And others we study because we are curious as to what makes them tick. Boris made me curious.

I put my family, parents, grandparents, and other relatives and celebrities, including writers, ahead of Boris when it comes to admiration. But I liked the cut of his jib. Boris Yeltsin wasn't afraid to make changs. Could he have been ahead of his time? The Russian economy had to be in some kind of chaos after the breakup of the USSR, that seemed like the perfect time to reinvent Mother Russia. Yeltsin had too many hard liners working against him. But as my dad used to say, "In order to have any chance, you have to try."

Imagining this story drifted over a couple of decades before it came together. I picked the Eagle Ridge location because we happened to be living there at the time. Most of the Eagle Ridge locations do exist, except for the home on Pinehurst Drive. One more thought, Boris Yeltsin and his family were the only real figures in the story.

If you have an opinion you'd like to share, let me know at jprobideaux.com.

# Acknowledgments

To my wife Lorrie who keeps me moving forward with my writing. There's no encouragement like that from a full-blooded Italian. Ashli, my wonderful step-daughter, for her marketing and communication expertise, and Brian, my son-in-law and co-editor, proud parents to Luna and London who call us Nana and Papa. Many thanks to relatives and friends who laughed at the Boris premise for the last few years. And to, Rick, a new editor, who helped in so many ways with his creative lens and strong wit. Kevin in Seattle is a gifted resource that deserves recognition for the cover design and layout: he makes a very complicated process flow easily. Jon at Latah Publishing for his consult and wisdom and Sister Florence Leone who, as my teacher in the 5th grade, encouraged me to read in order to learn. Thanks to you all, especially Boris, our fictional ex-neighbor.